Dr. C. Lillefisk's
SIRENOLOGY

A GUIDE TO MERMAIDS & OTHER
UNDER-THE-SEA-PHENOMENA

To all in search of mermaids—you won't
find what you don't go looking for.

DR. C. LILLEFISK'S SIRENOLOGY
A Guide to Mermaids & Other Under-the-Sea-Phenomena

Published by Eye of Newt Books Inc. · www.eyeofnewtpress.com
Eye of Newt Books Inc. 56 Edith Drive, Toronto, Ontario, M4R 1C3

Library and Archives Canada Cataloguing in Publication

Title: Dr. C. Lillefisk's sirenology : a guide to mermaids & other under-the-sea phenomena / Jana
  Heidersdorf.
Other titles: Doctor C. Lillefisk's sirenology | Sirenology
Names: Heidersdorf, Jana, author, illustrator.
Description: Includes bibliographical references.
Identifiers: Canadiana 20230501575 | ISBN 9781777791865 (hardcover)
Subjects: LCSH: Mermaids. | LCSH: Mermaids—Folklore. | LCSH: Mermaids—Mythology. | LCGFT:
  Illustrated works.
Classification: LCC GR910 .H54 2023 | DDC 398.4/5—dc23

ISBN: 978-17777918-6-5

10 9 8 7 6 5 4 3 2 1

Printed in China

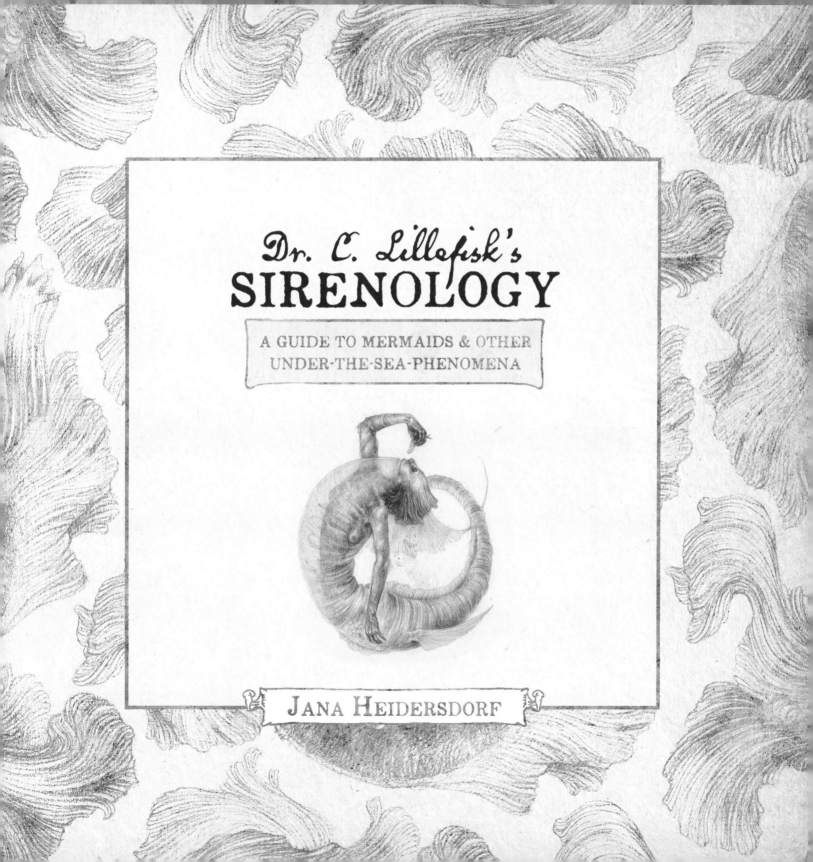

Dr. C. Lillefisk's
SIRENOLOGY

A GUIDE TO MERMAIDS & OTHER
UNDER-THE-SEA-PHENOMENA

JANA HEIDERSDORF

TABLE *of* CONTENTS.

MIDNIGHT ZONE

LAKE ZONE

RIVER ZONE

INTRODUCTION

Some people believe we grow out of fairy tales. That it's natural. Like losing baby teeth, it's something we just must do. Shedding fairy tales is like a marker of adulthood, a badge to pin on our lapel before we go to work at our adult job, doing adult-job things like staring at the bubbles of the water cooler and contemplating the meaning of our grey and joyless life. It is my assertion that fairy tales have been baked into our bones. We cannot grow out of them. They grow with us as we spin new ones, new stories, our own and others', and weave them into one big story we call our life. Reality.

Our brains make meaning. Our brains make stories. And if we try to deny ourselves this wonderful capacity, if we decide to rid our perception of all these rich layers of meaning, strip it down to the naked truth—we blind ourselves. We deny creativity and progress. If we cannot imagine anything but what lies right in front of our eyes, we shrink our world. Instead, let's wonder "what if?" and open portals to new possibilities and understandings. Fairy tales are seedlings for the wild and fearless imaginings that build our future.

The truth is, we need fairy tales to see what is right in front of our eyes. You need to believe a twig can be alive to see the stick insect among the shrubbery. If we pride ourselves on shedding the fairies, what happens when we meet a creature we know only from myth? We decide it cannot be real, prefer to fault our own perception over our belief in what is and is not possible. That would be tragic. To find something novel and reject it because embracing it would require an admission of not-knowing or (dare I say) being wrong.

As someone who has spent her career searching for mermaids and documenting my findings, as someone working tirelessly to convince fellow academics, fellow scientists, and the gatekeeping institutions that make funding decisions that my work is not a childish fantasy, I can tell you this tragedy is truth. Most minds, even the most brilliant ones, pivot around what is already known. There is no room for perceiving something just beyond understanding. Even those who have joined me in my search still doubt, but they have joined me because their willingness to forge ahead towards something novel burns brighter than doubt.

Let me tell you: Those who set out to find mermaids, do indeed find them. Those sitting in their dusty studies, dissecting my research and theses, every thread of evidence presented, with their nay-saying—well, they will never experience the excitement of witnessing an adolescent *Gorgóna gorgóna* nurturing its serpents.

By sharing my findings with you, by publishing this journal, I want to encourage you to go out into the world and search for your own mermaids. (Please ensure safety measures are in place! Some mermaids are dangerous or live in treacherous environments.) Go out into the wilderness and keep your eyes open. Watch the streams, wade into the oceans. Listen to the calls on the wind and mind where you step. Marvel at the beauty presented by these creatures alive on Earth with us. And as you observe your first mermaid, however it may appear to you—and it will likely be beyond anything you've imagined!—remember that it is our duty to protect them and their habitats. It is up to humans to preserve this planet that we all share. And it is *for* us as well. For what greater loneliness could there be than being trapped on this planet with only humans for company? Go forth and seek out mermaids. Fall in love and share that love because it is within that love that stewardship and empathy can be found.

I love mermaids and hope to make you fall in love with them as well. As you may notice in the perusal of my journal, much of my research is incomplete. There is work to be done in the field of sirenology if I want to make a convincing case for mermaids to be recognized by scientific and political authorities. And they need to be if we want to protect them and their habitats in any meaningful way.

Finally, I wish to address a selfish matter: I need support. There is so much more to discover within the world of the mermaids; I want to be able to communicate with them and learn how they see the world. I want to know more. I want to do more. One feels helpless nowadays, like a tiny *Serra repere*, paddling against the rushing stream of a river, and it is an unfortunate requirement of our world that to make a big splash, one needs money. My equipment, my travels: They require funding. Funds have always been difficult to procure as my research has been scorned and ignored rather than seen as an opportunity for discovery. But now we know how symbiotic the relationship between humans and the global ecosystem is. I implore you to fund this humble scientist working on exploring the wonders of the natural world. Fund my mission of discovery and awe; fund beauty, connection, and understanding; fund fairy tales because within them might lie hope for humanity. Fund mermaids.

It is my hope that the proceeds from this book will enable me to upgrade my equipment and allow me to follow new and promising leads. It is my hope that the publication of these preliminary findings will raise awareness of my work and the creatures at its centre. If you wish to support my research and join me in my quest for mermaids, please reach out to me or my publisher. Or simply spread the word. Every whisper helps.

A NOTE ON ORGANIZATION & CATEGORIZATION

I have given much thought to the arrangement of my findings in this book. Would you meet each mermaid as I did, their order determined by my travels and the instance of discovery? An exact replica of my journal wouldn't be possible as my handwriting is quite illegible, and my notes written in haste and excitement tend to be jumbled, as if you were looking straight into my head. Think about somebody looking into your head when you haven't had the time to tidy up—the thoughts are all over the place. Instead, I have decided to preserve some of the immediacy and authenticity of my journal while giving this publication the shape of something useful and perhaps entertaining. This book presents my research after a good spring cleaning.

The first distinction I wish to mention is that of the phenomena. As I have spent more and more time in the world of the mermaids, I have come to realize that some of my observations were most likely naturally occurring phenomena in the mermaid world and not distinct mermaids themselves. Some phenomena I have found a deeper understanding of, but for others, I have barely scratched the surface of what there is to know. I also need to acknowledge that some phenomena may turn out to be mermaid species after all and vice versa. Science and its servants are not infallible, and sirenology is a field where much of the foundational knowledge is still missing.

Further, you may notice that not all mermaids share the same genus. This is mainly due to my own hubris. I have parsed patterns in how different species may be related based on geography, appearance, and behaviours. This categorization is, if anything, a very tentative first approach to finding potential coherences within mermaidkind. In general, you will find most mermaids belonging to the genus *Serra*, some to the genus *Sirena*, a few to that of *Gorgóna*, and one *Sedna*. I will, however, for simplicity's sake, refer to all as mermaids or sirens interchangeably.

Finally, I have decided to order the mermaids based on where you may encounter them, not by geography, but by the mermaid's habitat: salt water or fresh water. Within the saltwater habitats, the distinctions are made by depth: sunlight zone, twilight zone, and midnight zone. Within the freshwater habitats, the distinctions are made between lakes and rivers. Of course, many mermaids are not bound by our human categories, so you may see a mermaid who commonly lives in the midnight zone driven to the water's surface for one reason or another. Some may even change their habitat over their life cycle.

Please do not consider this lone scientist's journal as the infallible authority of sirenology. Think of it as you would think of the writings of early healers, apothecaries, or natural philosophers, wise people limited by the knowledge of their time, important building blocks on the way to true enlightenment. I do not wish to diminish my own findings; I wish to express my hope in how much further our knowledge and understanding of mermaids will grow in the coming decades. I wish to be one of the first dedicating their life to this worthy effort. If I call myself Paracelsus, it is only in my fervent belief that there will also be a Darwin or a Galileo of sirenology in our future.

Sunlight Zone

SALTWATER
MERMAIDS &
PHENOMENA

I can only imagine
how abscondita's additional
eyes factor into its experience of the world.

SERRA
Abscondita

At first, all that's seen are six perfect pearls buried in the sand—arranged neatly in a row, largest to smallest. They shine and they twinkle and sometimes they blink. Upon closer inspection, the hidden shape, the impression of an eel-like body under the sand materializes. The creature twitches away, swirling up silt and sand to mask its escape; it was watching you with those pale eyes. This is what it is like to meet your first mermaid. It may not be what you expected, but is exhilarating all the same.

After weeks of studying *Serra abscondita* both in its habitat and in my lab, I can confirm not all its six eyes—located only on the left side of its body—perform the same function. The most prominent eye, the largest and first in line, is most useful in the detection of predators as it has an abundance of rods that allow it to perceive even minute changes in light, whether it may be the shadow of a hungry seagull circling high in the air or a sirenologist blocking out the sun. Where this first eye has mostly rods, the second eye has mostly cones and specializes in the perception of movements. While this may warn *abscondita* of danger, it primarily alerts the mermaid to prey—crabs and small fish—in its vicinity. The high number of cones in this eye means this mermaid can likely see a spectrum of colour, if not the one humans are used to. Ultraviolet, for example, is visible to many sea creatures as it makes zooplankton easy to spot, while light with shorter wavelengths, such as red, is swallowed as the water increases in depth.

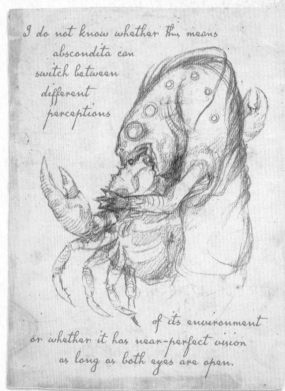

I do not know whether this means abscondita can switch between different perceptions

of its environment or whether it has near-perfect vision as long as both eyes are open.

The purpose of *abscondita*'s dominant eyes is clear. However, the function of the others is less so. They are each equipped with a tapetum lucidum, a layer of tissue reflecting available light back through the retina. As this is a typical adaptation for nocturnal creatures or fish of the deep sea, it is puzzling for a mermaid at home in the shallow waters of the Mediterranean and suggests a period in early development during which *abscondita* dwelt in deeper waters, perhaps to avoid predation. Notably, these eyes remain lidded during the day (the lid a milky, pearlescent film) but open at night even as the mermaid is seemingly asleep. Does this mean a part of *abscondita*'s sensory system remains awake at all times?

PHENOMENON
Caeruleus

I discovered a curious phenomenon that I have called *caeruleus* in a small group of mermaids washed up on the Hawaiian shoreline. They may have been *Gorgóna vela*, though it was difficult to tell for sure as their dorsal fins had already started to disintegrate. Once I arrived at the scene, I found the mermaids, most of them already dead, illuminating the night with a blue light. Only the living ones were still a yellowish brown. This change in colour is the phenomenon named *caeruleus* for the cerulean pallor these creatures have in death. In the time I had to observe the last living mermaids, I tracked how the blue spread through their bodies, starting with the intestines and reaching out through to their extremities. The longest death took 124 minutes. By then, the entire body had turned bright blue and continued to glow for six more hours until it decomposed rapidly into an acidic, gooey substance, which unfortunately is the only state in which I was able to preserve any remains.

According to my observations, *caeruleus* serves as a physiological indicator of a mermaid's imminent death, either as a warning to other individuals or as a last resort of the immune system. Still, I am left with more questions than answers. What exactly caused this reaction? Does it signal the natural end to a life cycle, or one brought on by a certain pollutant or illness? Is it simply a sign or the cause of death? And does this phenomenon occur in all species of mermaid? The only thing I am sure about is how much research still lies ahead of me.

The mermaid appears restful, leading me to think that caeruleus occurs without pain.

An observational
sketch of the blue
spreading through the
mermaid's body, starting
with the intestines.

❧ PHENOMENON ❧
Draconis.

These mermaids wear the skins of dragons. Or at least, that's what I first thought. When the discarded hulls of *draconis* were found, I assumed an undiscovered mermaid had shed its skin, which would have been exciting in its own way. Imagine! The form of the discard, however, raised many questions. There were arms, a torso, and a long tail, but no dactyls or face, and I therefore concluded that this discard was more like clothing or a hull. Of course, the notion of clothing for mermaids is highly contentious. If you wish to be hounded by stern, dismissive letters for the entire length of your career, merely suggest the possibility at a symposium. Therefore, I will not in any way liken the phenomenon of *draconis* to our own human habit of creating clothing, costume, or armour. Instead, I propose the shell I discovered to be not unlike that of a hermit crab, as it has, at some point, housed a mermaid; indeed, it has been been *worn*. In all likelihood, the creature slowly transformed itself, cobbling together an outer shell from the corpses and discards of deep-sea creatures living, extinct, and still unknown to us. These shells are held together by a sticky secretion, likely provided by the mermaid itself and contributing to the preservation of the organic matter. Thankfully, I was able to obtain some samples, and further investigation should help to confirm its nature.

If you're lucky you can find a preserved dragon skin in a natural history museum near you.

Despite my best efforts, I have yet to catch a living specimen to answer my many questions. Does it wear this additional skin as a deterrent or is it a way to survive corrosive conditions? Do I dare to speculate on the possibility of a spiritual or cultural aspect of this behaviour? The idea is so tantalizing I am willing to risk another accusing letter from Archibald, that old naysayer. There is a whole world beneath the waves that is just out of reach. Even having dedicated my life to the study of sirenology, I must accept I will only ever breach the surface of understanding.

A sample of draconis secretion.

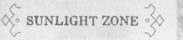
SIRENA
Dugon

Naturally, one of the first places I visited on my journey into the world of the mermaids was Australia. It is here that the highest population of dugongs, creatures that have long been linked to mermaids, reside. Their Latin name, *Sirenia*, which means sea cow, is at the root of the word *Sirena*, giving an entire genus its name. The dugong looks as though it has the tail of a whale with the top of a walrus. Additionally, it is the only herbivorous mammal that spends all its life in the sea—or so I had originally thought before I realized that some among the dugong are indeed *Sirena* and not *Sirenia*.

For careful observers, it is easy to spot *Sirena dugon* by looking for dugongs with more than one juvenile, which is a rare occurrence. The *dugon* spends most of its life in a seemingly juvenile state. Though not naturally born from the dugong, this mermaid subsists on the milk of a dugong mother. The *dugon* waits for a female dugong about to give birth, shadowing

An actual juvenile dugong.

the sea cow through the shallow coastal waters, which requires some, but not much, stealth. She smears the mother's feces over herself by rolling in it to ensure it smells familiar when the mother finally gives birth. Taking advantage of the dugong's weak eyesight and their usual birth rate of just one calf per pregnancy, the *dugon* moves in and joins the new family. The mermaid doesn't grow as a usual calf would and so can only remain with its foster "mother" for about eighteen months, during lactation.

One of the many curious things about this mermaid is that the creature is fully mature, yet still surviving by acting as a babe. I suspect that at around age sixty, the *dugon* carries its own offspring to full term and finds them a proper dugong foster parent, restarting the cycle. It is difficult to say whether this is a parasitic or a symbiotic relationship. How would the dugongs benefit from the *dugon*? Are they less tempting to predators if they look greater in number? Sharing a mother's milk with a second calf is usually not desirable, but perhaps the relationship between the calf and the *dugon* itself should not be dismissed lightly. A newborn calf living with, and learning from, a sibling potentially over five decades older would teach the dugong calf a wisdom unknown to other newborns. I look forward to returning to these warm, aquamarine shores so that I might better study the interrelationships between *dugon* and dugong.

Note the physiological
differences, particularly
the dactyls in place of flippers.

⊰ GORGÓNA ⊱

Eucrante

O n a covert little beach on Milos, an island in Greece, I studied the *Gorgóna eucrante*. At first this creature might be disappointing as, upon surface-level observation, this species seems rather mundane. It looks the way an old sailor might have described a mermaid: half woman, half fish. As a scientist of sirenology, however, I hunkered down on this beautiful beach to study this mermaid beyond its fairy tale appearance.

I do also wonder if a eucrantes' hair is part of this species' courtship rituals.

To my delight, I discovered *eucrante* is a social creature. They spend their youth in family units within a larger community, seeking strength and security in numbers. This inevitably leads to individuals staying in contact with each other throughout most of their adult lives. One of their more fascinating sociocultural traits is the use of their hair in catching prey. Mentored by older *eucrantes*, a young mermaid learns how to braid and weave its hair into a successful fishing net. Variations in net designs are passed on through bloodlines, with specific traits like hair colour or density encouraging different styles of knots and braiding patterns, even suggesting family identifiers within those styles.

Further, I have been able to observe a use of gestures—which incorporate their hair, facial, arm, and tail expressions—to an extent that deserves to be recognized as a language understood within the whole *eucrantes* species with dialectal variations depending on the location and family. There doesn't seem to be an interest in communicating with humans, as with the *will-o-the-wisps*, but there is perhaps potential.

Nevertheless, akin to *homo sapiens*, much of *Gorgóna eucrantes'* behaviours suggest "culture" in the human sense of the word. These creatures could be a window into understanding and unlocking how we study and engage with sirens across genera.

SERRA
Exercitus

Meet the smallest, yet fiercest mermaid species I've discovered so far. Despite its size of less than ten centimetres, this *Serra* is a menace in the water and a danger in any airspace up to ten metres above the ocean. The potential damage *Serra exercitus* can inflict on animals many times its size is disproportional. With its strong jaws, it effortlessly tears pieces of flesh from its prey, each wound round like a penny and harmless on its own; yet what a swarm of several hundred tiny *exercitus* leaves behind could fill a handbag. Swarms of *exercitus* can hunt down larger swimming prey, like a manta ray or a sunfish, as I have observed them doing on occasion. More often, though, they turn their greedy eyes towards trawlers and their conveniently filled nets. Besides robbing fishers of their livelihood, this newly established habit comes with an increasing willingness of *exercitus* to seek other ships, or any sea craft, which leads to unfortunate accidents with motorboats unable to outrun these flying pests and pleasure cruisers surprised by mermaids flapping onto the deck, snapping at ankles and toes, before diving back into the safety of the water.

Once, I witnessed a fight between two individuals and the outcome was expectedly lethal. At the end of the duel, both combatants were gravely injured, and as such, they were killed and eaten by the group. A mermaid carrying a disease or showing the first signs of *caeruleus*, on the other hand, leaves the swarm by its own volition and quickly dies of illness or predation. In this way, natural selection eliminated out much intraspecies aggression in favour of cooperation. The swarms consist of only the most focused and healthy individuals, ready to unload all their pent-up aggressive energy onto their prey.

It is difficult not to see a link between these creatures and our own human cunning.

In the case of exercitus the term "army" seems arguably more fitting than "swarm."

There are rumours of international military organizations showing a sudden interest in sirenology since the discovery of this species. This information is—like all rumours—to be taken with a grain of salt and likely originated during a late-night laboratory session when a careless zoologist lost an ear to an *exercitus* and declared it a biological weapon. Just to be clear—this hypothetical person was not me.

An exercitus is rarely alone, for it is in a group that it becomes a lethal threat.

10cm

Desert locust
(Schistocerca gregaria)

15cm

A jaw
specimen.

SIRENA
Exocoetus.

This mermaid resembles flying fish, which are its prey. Its similarity to its own food source makes it an especially successful hunter. Upon closer inspection, however, *Sirena exocoetus* is easy to distinguish from the flying fish primarily because of its long arms. Following its prey into the air, this mermaid lunges its arms forward to grab the unlucky fish. *Exocoetus'* teeth are small and pearly white, sharp enough to easily pierce scales. Together the mermaid and its prey splash back into the ocean. Interestingly, in one flock of *exocoetus*, I observed a frenzy so rabid that once the prey were nearly exterminated, the otherwise social creatures began hunting each other down until they reduced their numbers to one lone individual.

I followed this individual *exocoetus* for three days. It didn't seem hurried or harried, fat on its feed and champion of the flock. Eventually it came upon another school of flying fish being hunted by other *exocoetus* and joined them. Unfortunately, I was called away to follow another lead, but I must note how surprising it is to witness a species risking the extinction of its local population in favour of maintaining a balance between itself and its prey—whether by instinct or conscious decision I can only speculate. Though extreme, the *exocoetus'* measures seem successful, as currently, according to fisherman and zoologist accounts, both hunter and hunted flourish by practising similar survival strategies.

A group of exocoetus can easily decimate a school of flying fish in no time—I have seen it.

I would love to track an entire flock of this mermaid species to observe their individual movements and the changes in population. Unfortunately, most common tracking methods are unsuitable for subjects equipped with nimble fingers capable of removing any foreign object. My previous attempts at attaching GPS tracking devices to mermaids have proven so disastrous I simply cannot get funding for it anymore.

SERRA
Florentissimorum

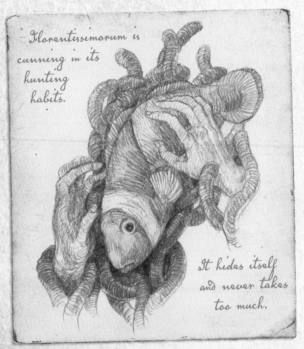

Florentissimorum is cunning in its hunting habits.

It hides itself and never takes too much.

Sea anemones are dangerous creatures—I have watched them lull fish into a false sense of security and then, one day, the fish is no longer, and the anemone is already luring in its next victim. What does a sea anemone whisper to its prey as it gently strokes it with venom and bites off its head? What does it murmur to the clownfish seeking shelter in its arms, its sole symbiotic protégé? Does it warn these fish, thinking themselves safe in their venomous habitat, of its sister, the deceiver with the face of a stranger?

Serra florentissimorum is a parasite on the symbiotic relationship between sea anemone and clownfish. *Florentissimorum* has the alien beauty of the anemone paired with the wily nature of humans. It lives hidden in the Pacific reefs and lagoons. The delicate shapes of its ornamental appendages allow it to blend in perfectly with the surrounding polyps. Its teeth are deadly to fish and crustaceans alike and it is immune to the venomous sting of the sea anemone, making it the single predator of the cnidarian and its little ecosystem of clownfish.

The mermaid is not greedy in its appetites and is careful not to scare away the entire fish population, but will occasionally snatch away an individual or two. The clownfish are reluctant to abandon their symbiotic lifestyle with the sea anemones and accept the mermaid as their shepherd. *Florentissimorum* weeds out weaker members of the flock, and in some instances, specifically targets the matriarch of the family, so another preferable candidate can take her place, therefore resulting in a new generation of fish more likely to learn or be born with behaviours more to the mermaid's liking.

SERRA
Glaucus.

Among ancient cultures there existed a belief that eating another creature's flesh could endow them with new abilities, with power, with a longer life. In truth, or so I thought, eating simply offers a full belly and much-needed nutrients. As humans, for instance, we do not absorb a wild boar's ferocity, a cow's pattern, or a rabbit's sensitive nose. Yet those ancient myths came to mind as I observed and documented *Serra glaucus.* Held adrift by gas-filled sacs located in the lower back and tail, *glaucus* spends all its energy on stalking exquisite prey: the incredibly toxic Portuguese man o' war and its less harmful cnidarian cousins. While their poison would act as a deterrent to other species, and is lethal to humans, this mermaid is immune.

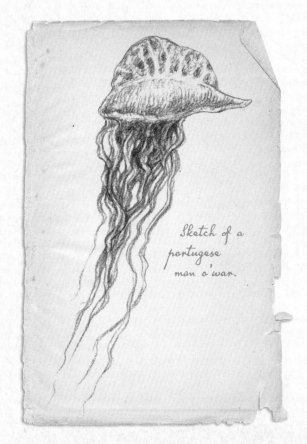

Sketch of a portugese man o' war.

Furthermore, I have noted that *glaucus* takes in the poisonous nematocysts of its prey, storing them in fingerlike growths protruding from its body. Its increasing potency is observable as the *glaucus* grows into maturity and confidence. Any creature daring to sink its fangs into this mermaid will be affected by a poison much more concentrated than the cnidarians'. *Glaucus* becomes less tasty with every meal. The knowledge that it is nigh untouchable surely soothes it while floating in the open sea, flaunting its colours as a warning sign. *Glaucus* swims close enough to the surface to breathe the air. With its brown and gold tinge, *glaucus* is hardly hidden from the hungry eyes above and below, but one can afford to be bold when one has become the most dangerous of them all.

PHENOMENON
Impetus

There is an exoparasite I've labelled *impetus*, in part because it is truly a rogue that feeds off mermaids but also because it inexorably alters the physique and behaviour of its victims. This creature looks alien, like a large leech with strong, stumpy arms ending in long claws and a sail-like dorsal fin indicating its preference for travelling close to the water's surface by catching the wind. Just like its prey, it has a long, graceful tail.

I was lucky to discover a specimen of *impetus* still clinging to the remains of the mermaid it had infested. Rarely am I lucky enough to have a specimen in such good condition to examine closely, especially as it seemed to survive without nourishment for several weeks—presumably a requirement for the parasite when searching for a new host to feed on. While it is less picky when it comes to the siren in question, *impetus* does require the blood of a mermaid to thrive. My attempts at substituting with different animals and even human blood were unfortunately unsuccessful.

This Gorgóna eucrante, is a species with a long torso akin to that of a human's in size.

A healthy *impetus* weighs about ten pounds, not an inconsiderable burden for a mermaid to carry on its back. If the host has its own dorsal fin, the first days of infestation are particularly hard as *impetus* will partially eat it, partially tear it out, and the remains will ultimately die off under the pressure of its body. If this early period does not lead to infection or attract the attention of a predator, the mermaid's chances of survival increase significantly. Further, I have observed that *impetus* can control the mermaid's movements and direction by inflicting pressure and pain on either the left or right side where its claws hold fast. Depending on the host's ability to adapt to its new circumstances, the subsequent swimming impairment and potential shift to the sunlight zone is often more dangerous than the blood leeched by the *impetus*. The fine droplets consumed through its proboscis are probably not even noticed by most hosts. I suspect the average mermaid survives only a year with *impetus* latched onto it, even if a much longer life might be possible under ideal conditions.

Impetus needs these long
digits to properly latch on with
its whole body.

Sirena latentem in its natural habitat waiting for prey to swim by.

SIRENA
Latentem

The spider, a widely admired creature, is a bug that holds a place near and dear to my heart. There is no shortage of spiders aboard ships, which is where I have spent most of my life these past five years. I have discovered a peculiar mermaid who has adopted a way of hunting that resembles my favourite silk-spinning arachnid. Most *Sirena latentem* have two arms and two legs connected by a membrane that gives it a disc-like appearance, while some *latentem* have a more fish-like fin in place of the leg-like limbs. While its arms and legs, or tail, are rather stumpy and inflexible, its fingers and toes are nimble and strong, despite their delicate appearance. This helps *latentem* to find grip in its hunting grounds: coral reefs and rocky areas with a high density of caves and crevices. Typically, this mermaid hunts by anchoring its claws in two opposite walls of stone or organic matter, stretching its body and fins like a net, stuck fast and waiting for its next meal to bump into it.

This latentem's nearly transluscent fins spread like a web ready to ensnare its prey.

Small creatures are guided directly into its mouth by the movements of its body and membrane, to be swallowed whole. To entrap larger prey, the mermaid lets go of its handholds and curls up around it, creating a cocoon. Then it ejects stomach acids (to which it is immune) and proceeds to dissolve its prey bit by bit. The lower half of its face is elastic and can stretch around prey up to half its size. Four deep-set teeth keep its catch in place until it stops struggling. The ring muscles responsible for swallowing guide it further down the throat and into the stomach, where it is dissolved by gastric acids.

Its fins are extraordinary limbs. They are highly sensitive and allow for *latentem* to feel even the most subtle movements in the surrounding water. Since this mermaid is not particularly fast or acrobatic, this warning system is crucial in allowing for early reactions—whether it be to rearrange its trap or flee dangerous predators. Should the need arise to flee, although the rat-sized *latentem* are known to overestimate their ample devouring abilities, it will let itself drift upwards, carried by its own swim bladder, until the danger has passed. Sometimes *latentem* will make good use of the opportunity and hitch a ride to a new hunting ground by jumping onto a larger marine creature.

SIRENA
Medusa Clara

It can be dangerous to turn an ancient place of ritual and mystery into a tourist attraction. The underwater cave systems of the Yucatán cenotes in Mexico, once a Mayan sacrificial site, are now a popular destination for diving and relaxing. Yet even today these flooded caves remain, in parts, unexplored. They harbour archaeological wonders, and they harbour ghosts of the past.

If it were not for the soft bioluminescent glow of its body, *Sirena medusa clara* would be nearly invisible. Its photophore eyes are the only indicator of its presence, two beacons glowing in the dark and leading any diver stung by its long, toxic tentacles astray. Its venom induces dreamlike hallucinations, keeping its hapless victims in a state of blissful confusion until they drown. Even victims lucky enough to escape *medusa clara*'s hungry embrace eventually choose to return, seeking the high of its potent drug despite the risk of a lethal outcome.

The case of *medusa clara* has been particularly interesting to observe, not because of the mermaid itself, but for the way humans have reacted to its existence. Various companies have put in serious effort to lay hands on a sample of its venom. At the same time, a cult has formed around *medusa clara*, the members willing to risk their lives in the hope of experiencing its addictive touch. For others, diving into its territory has become a popular sport, something done on a dare or a whim.

Tentacles processed into yarn are woven into clothes to carry out assassinations.

In this humble researcher's opinion, one should be glad *medusa clara* only takes its toll after a digestion period of several months, otherwise the caves would devour these wanton visitors like a black hole. So far, only a small number of those in search of *medusa clara* were successful in getting themselves killed.

Due to its gelatinous body, this mermaid is hard to locate and even harder to catch. Pliable enough to squeeze through the narrowest rocky crevices, tunnels, and fangs of any predator foolish enough to challenge it, *medusa clara* is lethal, tempting, and elusive. Do not seek it out.

SERRA
Pharynx.

Serra pharynx's tail and body are covered in glorious, luminescent scales that shimmer like precious metals, making mother-of-pearl seem dull in comparison. When the fractured light shining down through the waves reflects off the mermaid's body, it becomes difficult to tell whether *pharynx* is truly there or whether one's eyes are playing tricks with the water and light, creating only a shimmering illusion.

It is not difficult to understand why *pharynx* are hunted for their scales and worth a fortune on the black market. While most scales and skins a collector may come across are retrieved from the sea floor—old, scratched things—there are still poachers bringing in whole, beautiful specimens. It is possible that within only a few years this mermaid will be extinct, even though *pharynx* is a vicious predator that can scare off even the most daring diver. When money is on the table, human lives are cheap, the call of fortune superseding reason.

With a remarkable aptitude for stillness, *pharynx* lurks patiently in crevices, the shadows turning its scales a translucent grey, and waits for prey and predators to pass. Having been fortunate enough to witness *pharynx* in all its glory, I still have trouble believing how near invisible it can become. When it ambushes a fish or an unfortunate hand, *pharynx* does so in a flash of silver and rainbow. It is a beautiful spectacle, though its victims may think otherwise

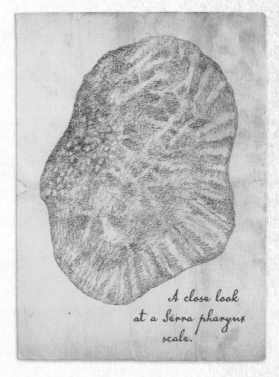

A close look at a Serra pharynx scale.

as the sharp teeth of its outer oral jaws fasten onto them. *Pharynx*'s jaw is a vice, its external teeth hold its prey while its inner pharyngeal jaws shoot forward and tear at the unfortunate victim. The mechanics are brutal, but effective, and in this scientist's objective opinion, a justified end to any poacher caught this way. Indeed, most divers still hunting for *pharynx* can be recognized by distinctive disfigurements and missing limbs.

If you, too, have fallen under the spell of *pharynx* scales, may I suggest you seek out one of the delicate fabrications made from mother-of-pearl and precious metals instead of the real thing?

SERRA
Servata.

This mermaid is a traveller, one who carries fresh food and company everywhere it goes. The sturdy membrane spanning the body of *Serra servata* from its tail to the delicate strings of bone and cartilage of its lower jaw forms a perfect prison for fish and even tiny mermaids like *Serra repere*. Indeed, I suspect *servata* of lying in wait at the base of freshwater tributaries waiting for little *repere* to fall into the oceanic trap. Captured prey and even a small reservoir of fresh water can stay within the membrane for years until it is devoured. Yet even without convenient arrangements such as the *repere*'s life cycle, *servata* is a passable hunter that can sustain itself without touching its passengers for a good while. I have concluded that *servata* can develop a fondness for particular inmates of its food storage.

Servata manipulating a fish through its jaw membrane.

Servata maintains the creatures in its membrane like a garden, supplying food and what appears to be general care and concern for these creatures' wellbeing, including short intervals of what I can only call play. I assume this activity not only serves the mermaid's amusement but constitutes a form of exercise for the fish and minute mermaids otherwise condemned to live in close quarters. Of course, this requires further research to confirm.

Despite *servata*'s care, the fish and mermaids generally do not thrive in captivity. They naturally lose muscle, and they lose the alertness that comes with living in the wild. If not already eaten by their fellow inmates, their bodies are removed and devoured during *servata*'s daily inspection of knocking and rubbing against the translucent container from the outside or fishing inside with its long dactyls. To make up for its inability to reach wholly into the storage sac, *servata* squeezes the membrane from the outside to force the chosen prey upwards where it can be reached with either hand or tongue. This action is a curious spectacle to behold. This behaviour has also been observed in relation to playing with the fish and petting them. I often wonder if *servata* and *repere* notice they are of the same family of creatures, and I would give everything for the opportunity to study the relationship of *servata* to other sirens in more depth.

SIRENA
Somniculosis

*T*he boat has run aground on a sandbank. A silhouette rises from the fog, swaying languidly in the breeze. A call, melodious yet feral, vibrates through the night air. Its mournful tone promises despair, casting an entrancing spell. The sailors recognize the maiden in need just as they recognize their own needs. Maybe they deserve some luck after all. It has been an ill-fated night, an ill-fated journey. Whatever the men may or may not have deserved, they were in for a surprise when attempting to interact with this "maiden." The folklore is all too easily conjured with *Sirena somniculosis*.

This mermaid is an adept ambush predator. It sets a trap for the unsuspecting and gullible human, for other manhunters, or for truly desperate creatures. *Somniculosis* simply needs to wait in the darkness, tail waving, and let out its long mournful cry. Somebody will come.

Based on the past prevalence of folk tales, it can be assumed that their population has dwindled throughout the last century, perhaps due to the common sailor becoming more selective in their breeding choices (or so my sources tell me). I have observed this creature lying in wait for a fortnight before it voyaged on to presumably more fruitful hunting grounds, proving that *somniculosis* still survive, their methods unchanged. It must therefore be deduced that the song of the *somniculosis* continues to find desperate ears—even if those happen nowadays to belong to *sirenologists*.

Somniculosis' lithe figure shrouded in darkness.

I am seeking a specimen to study further, as an examination of the the spine and tail of this mermaid would make a fascinating sirenological study exposing survival techniques and lure-hunting within the species.

SERRA
Torquem

One of the stranger-looking mermaids I have documented is *Serra torquem*. It is rather small and has many noteworthy features, such as spines on its tail, webbed dactyls, and its long, snapping tongue. It calls to mind the duck-billed platypus, a creature that seems caught between evolutionary changes. Still, *torquem* lives a simple life effortlessly drifting on the ocean's surface, lazily snapping at insects that catch its interest. It is kept aloft by a frilly membrane that spreads around it like a lifebuoy, bobbing up and down in the play of the waves. This frill catches, collects, and is decorated (so to speak) with kelp and seaweed, which create a sort of blanket of camouflage.

A sketch of torquem from above.

The spikes on *torquem*'s tail protect it from curious marine creatures that wonder at this floating mass of kelp, even though *torquem*'s most feared predators come from above: large ocean birds like albatrosses and sea eagles, but also the curious and plentiful seagulls. While the water itself can play tricks on the eyes of seafaring animals and can offer respite from birds and the sun, when the wind dies and the sea settles, *torquem* finds itself in trouble as the air-breathing mermaid cannot escape beneath the water's surface for long.

Marine birds such as the northern gannet are among torquem's primary predators.

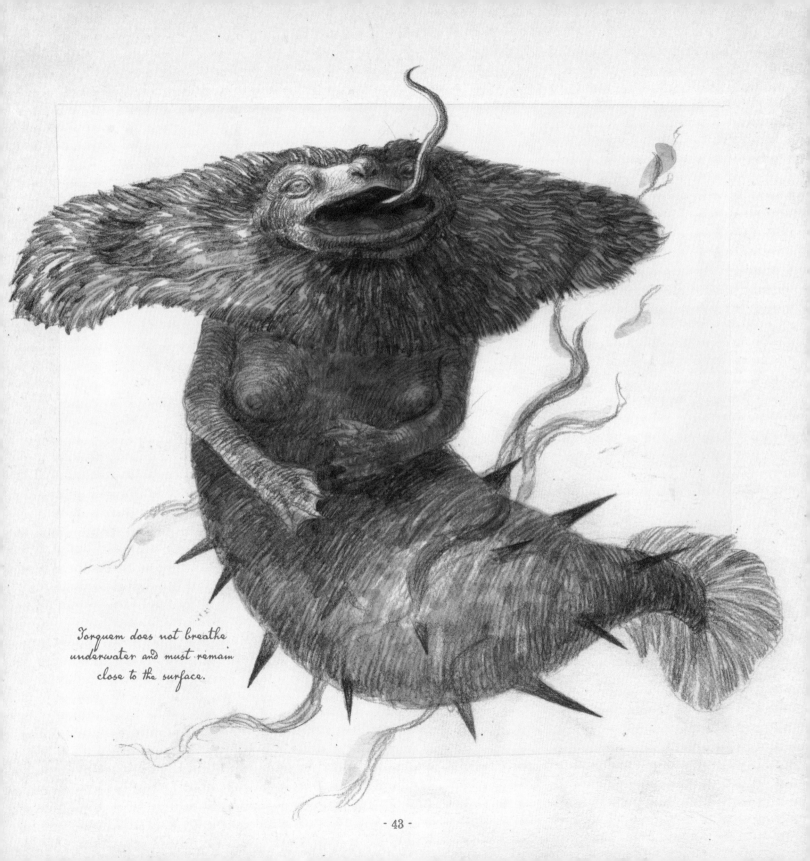

Torquem does not breathe
underwater and must remain
close to the surface.

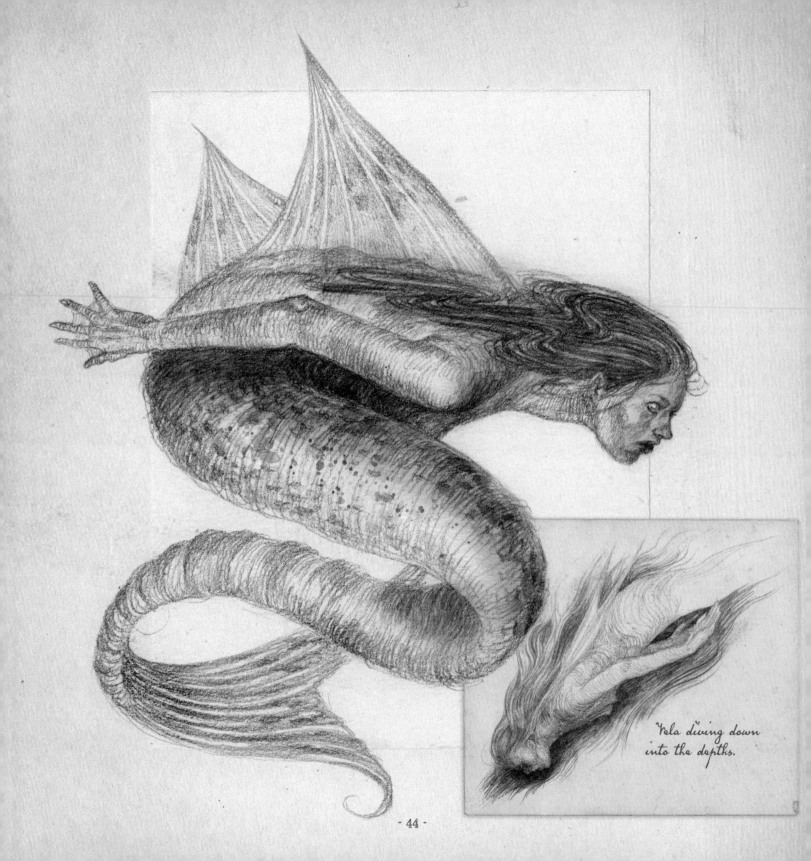

Vela diving down
into the depths.

⚜ GORGÓNA ⚜
Vela

The Sail

The Mussel

The Fan

The Wing

Whereas most of the *Gorgóna* inhabit the Mediterranean Sea, a few million years ago, some individuals of the genus must have made their way into the Atlantic Ocean, whether by choice or by happenstance. In this new environment, they developed a nomadic lifestyle, travelling long distances in shoals of five to eight individuals. I imagine they might have originally been looking for a new shoreline to settle, but for whatever reason, they kept to the open sea.

Over time this new habitat forced not only behavioural changes but also physiological ones. *Gorgóna vela* has grown a dorsal fin spanning its entire back, large enough to catch the wind when drifting at the surface and able to stabilize swimming manoeuvres when hunting for prey. Underwater, the sail can be folded back during deep dives to increase speed and agility.

After the discovery of *vela* I will need to keep an eye out for the occurrence of dorsal fins in other *Gorgóna* populations. Clearly, the required genetic material is slumbering somewhere in their DNA. And perhaps I have it all wrong and *vela* is the older species, *Sirena eucrante* and *Gorgóna*, only developing after a group got trapped in the Mediterranean. The elusive nature of both mermaids and research funding makes it difficult to draw definitive conclusions in sirenology. Most mermaid species reproduce slowly—which is in part why so many species are endangered—and many asexually, though *vela* notably do not. Either way, quite often every single individual is important for the survival of the species.

This is, in part, why it is so disturbing to have received reports of mermaid sails on the black market. Poaching for parts is a horrific human habit from which the world of sirens is not yet defended in the public courts. Please report any *vela* that you might spot on market streets or at online auctions so we can stop these atrocities.

Gorgóna vela dorsal fins come in several phenotypes.

- 45 -

SERRA
Vela Magna

*I*t is my assertion that this creature is indeed a mermaid, though perhaps one of the oldest species as its features have a prehistoric aesthetic and use to them. *Serra vela magna* has a set of four legs in addition to its tail. This alone would have my colleagues questioning this creature's clear siren ancestry. Unlike many mermaids, *vela magna* revels in the company of its extended family, swimming in groups of up to ten individuals.

Often, *vela magna* takes care of its offspring by carrying them on its back, safely tucked away behind a headplate of bone and cartilage. While the young are still too weak to swim on their own, their mother floats close to the ocean surface, paddling with her feet, and spreading her dorsal fin like a sail to catch the wind—hence *vela* in this creature's denomination. Indeed, similarity in behaviour and attributes to *Gorgóna vela* is evident; so much so, one could speculate that one is the far-off relative of the other. However, as we are missing the necessary genetic data, any such presumptions are nothing but speculation.

Sometimes a group of *vela magna* spends a prolonged time resting on a beach or sandbank, appearing to be more amphibious than most mermaid species. They dig shallow pits in the sand to accommodate the heavy trunks of their bodies. Young mermaids benefit from these moments of rest, as they are better at crawling over land than swimming in the sea, and they require the time to rest all their limbs and suck at their mother's teats.

Protective of her young, the mother does not dive or scavenge for food herself, so she relies on the childless members of the group to share their spoils with her. *Vela magna* are skilled swimmers and hunters despite their bulky appearance. The large dorsal fin can be pressed against their backs to create a sleek silhouette for speedy dives. Their tails are powerful tools both for swimming and defence. As travel companions, they take care of each other. If a mermaid is sick, infirm, or simply an unlucky hunter, it is fed and carried by the entire party. Once the offspring gain independence, they leave to create their own groups. Separate clusters recognize and greet one another in passing and sometimes join for a while. One wonders why so many mermaid species turned to solitude when observations of *vela magna* show such a harmonious life of cooperation and community.

Could mermaids be mammals who have returned to the sea?

Don't be silly, Cecilia.

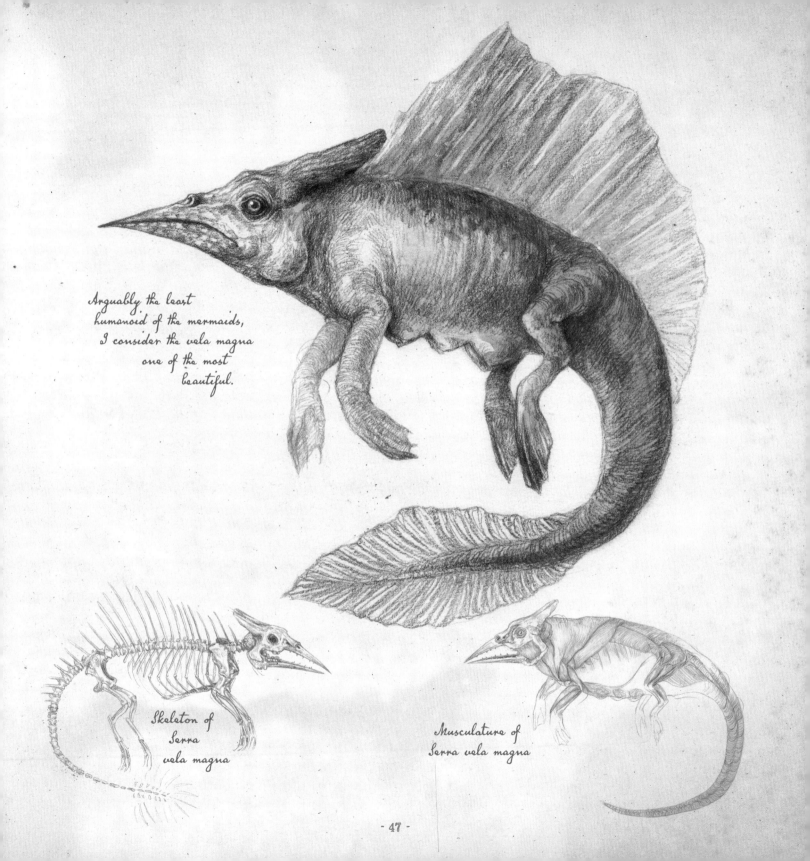

Arguably the least
humanoid of the mermaids,
I consider the vela magna
one of the most
beautiful.

Skeleton of
Serra
vela magna

Musculature of
Serra vela magna

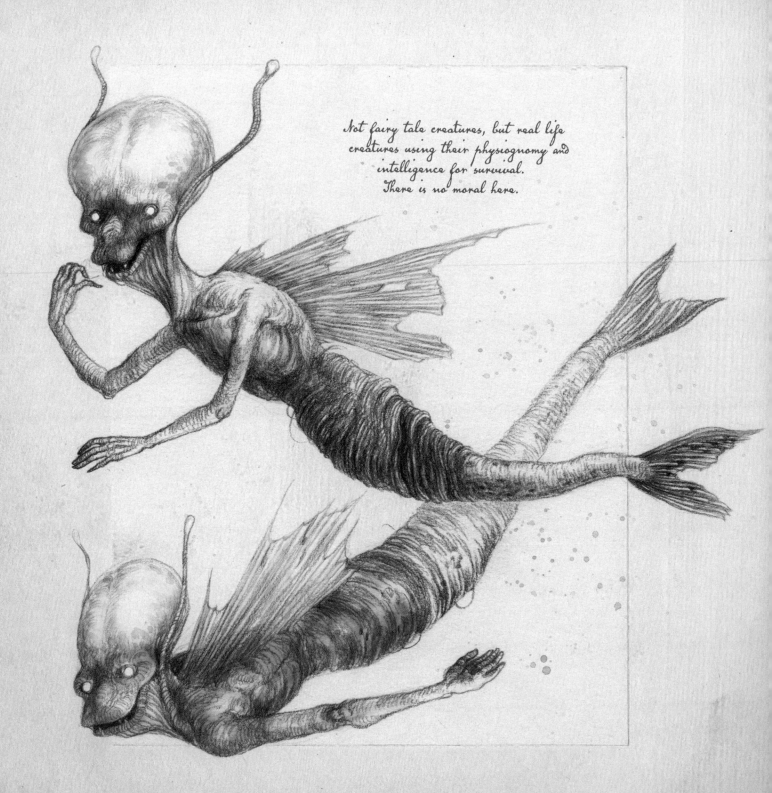

Not fairy tale creatures, but real life
creatures using their physiognomy and
intelligence for survival.
There is no moral here.

SIRENA
Will-o-the-wisp

They come in swarms, each one a torch drawing its prey further out to the sea. In pure darkness, it is easy to lose any sense of direction. Soon it becomes impossible to tell up from down, a dangerous position to hold in the depths. Thus the trap is set twofold as desperation has victims follow any light in the dim hope of reaching the surface and the sun again.

Will-o-the-wisps are not malicious or warlike like the *Serra macrourida* or *Serra exercitus*, rather they seem motivated by action and interaction. Like playful otters, they seem to find joy in interacting with one another and with a variety of species, including humans. If it is a quiet night, a person could find themselves surrounded by will-o'-the-wisps, each as bright as a lightbulb, and hear their clacking, cackling until they return to the dark to find a new playmate.

Will-o-the-wisps often work together to seduce creatures into their games. They are silly looking, and they act the part all so they are underestimated, shrugged off as a mere pest or annoyance. If I didn't know better than to project human traits onto the subjects of my studies, I might say they take pride or joy in luring large creatures off course. It is said they once led a blue whale astray.

These are the first species of mermaid I have found a way to successfully communicate with, which, as they have helpfully pointed out, reflects rather poorly on human intelligence. Indeed, the *will-o-the-wisps* reached out first, and it took a while to comprehend the signals their blinking lights were conveying. They speak in a sort of Morse code that I suspect was developed solely to engage with us humans. They have intimated they are not the only species of mermaid that can communicate beyond its own species, but they are the only one interested in humanity for more than just meat.

In our communications, they have revealed a more detailed account of their hunting methods. When their victim has swum so far it is weak and beyond help, they extinguish their lights and disperse, then tackle their prey from all sides. First only brushing against it—ever so softly—before starting to take bites: The great nibbling commences!

These intelligent, curious creatures have physically eluded me and my equipment. I have yet to actually see one of the swift, agile creatures myself, though I have spent enough time near a school of them to learn the light-sign language they have created. Every image that I have captured has been blurry, so here I present to you sketches constructed from what I know about their silhouettes, behaviours, and charming personalities.

Twilight Zone

SALTWATER
MERMAIDS &
PHENOMENA

❧ PHENOMENON ❧
Communia .

Imagine you could become a mermaid and all you needed to do was to take a scaled partner for life, one with a wide maw and a spacious gullet. This newfound species of fish, a larger cousin of the half-blind goby, has diminished sight and seeks the symbiotic companionship of others in order to survive. Whether this strange joining of fish and mermaid can be considered a new species or whether both the gobiiform and the *Sirena* have changed significantly enough to be considered subtypes of their origin species is yet to be determined. Thus far, all observed occurrences of *communia*—which is what I have decided to call this phenomenon until it can be conclusively matched with a species—involve a mermaid with a physical impairment (malformed tail, unwebbed dactyls etc.) and the blind gobiiform. If the mermaid joined in *communia* ever had a fully developed tail, it degenerates into a small paddle, not strong enough to propel its own body through the water, yet suitable to give the gobiiform directions by applying pressure to its insides. It is evident that both halves of this creature would perish on their own, but in joining they gain survivability. Their symbiotic life is not everlasting. I once tracked down a form of *communia* of which the mermaid half was in the late stages of *caeruleus*. While this condition leaves no corpse behind to examine, this case granted me access to a living specimen of the *communia gobiiform*, if only for a short while.

In my efforts to keep it alive, I tried feeding it food not yet processed by a mermaid's gastrointestinal tract, and it grew sick and feeble within days. This has led me to believe the fish may have grown dependent on consuming mermaid excrement. Later tests identified an unknown substance in the mermaid's feces retrieved from the gobiiform's stomach lining, which I suspect to have addictive qualities.

View of the mermaid's remaining tail.

How the gobiiform and its passenger have melded so they must live as one remains inexplicable at this time. I hesitate to even publish my research on this phenomenon for fear it might encourage the hunting of these fish for the purposes of joining with them or for uncovering a science so alien to us it might as well be magic. Please leave the study of these creatures to those of us who know what we are doing. To be an expert requires actual expertise, knowledge, and scientific truth—it cannot simply be wished into existence. Believe me, should new findings arise, I will share them through the proper channels in the hopes that it will benefit mermaidkind, a genus I specialize in and am very fond of.

SIRENA
Fiji

The Fiji Mermaid, named after its place of origin, was first exhibited in 1842 in P.T. Barnum's American Museum in New York. Naturalists at the time recognized it as a true—if ugly—mermaid and modern scholars of sirenology would have been wise to trust their judgment. Instead, we were fooled by the many copies populating the sideshows in the wake of Barnum's success. After the original's disappearance in the 1860s, they were the only specimens left for dissection and proved to be no more than the torsos of juvenile monkeys sewn on top of fish tails. With the original mermaid presumed lost to a fire and all supposed rediscoveries turning out to be nothing more than further acts of animal cruelty to indulge the masses and fill pockets with coin, what was there for rational minds to do but declare the Fiji Mermaid a hoax?

A depiction of Barnum's mermaid.

Famous grifter P.T. Barnum actually did discover a real mermaid.

Oh, scientists should have pursued the truth of the matter! We should have continued to dig through the hundreds of fakes to find one true mermaid. For once, we should have exchanged our skepticism for hope, the hope of living in a world more magical for having mermaids in it. Fortunately, the magic in this world has a way to make itself known if you are only willing to look. I have discovered a body like that of Barnum's Fiji Mermaid washed up on a beach on Yasawa Island. This specimen is beyond a doubt of the *Sirena* family. Due to our own neglect, we have learned next to nothing about what I would call *"Sirena Fiji"* in the decades since its initial discovery. I can only hope for this new find to convince my narrow-minded colleagues this creature is a *Sirena* worth investigating further.

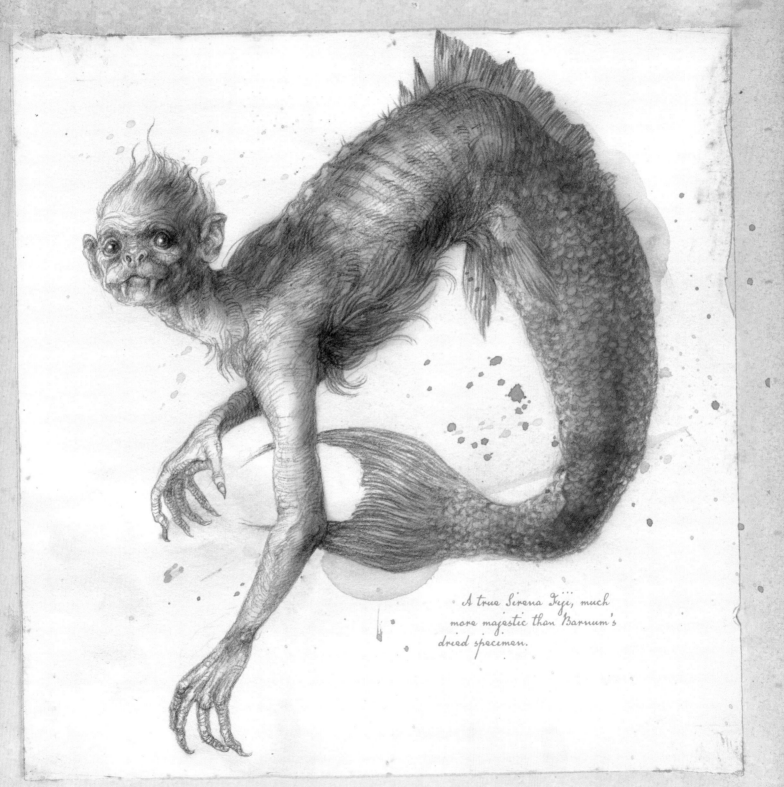

A true Serena Fiji, much
more majestic than Barnum's
dried specimen.

The mandibles of *filis*
are incredibly strong.

❧ SIRENA ❧
Filis

Nature has shaped *Sirena filis* into a formidable ambush predator. A quick, capable swimmer with excellent vision, it is not easily evaded. However, what makes it especially dangerous is its ability to combine wits with physical prowess. Whether from the shadows or mid-chase, *filis* whips its tentacles forward with lethal precision to wrap around the fleeing prey. This mermaid primarily eats fish, but *filis* is not a picky eater. Shrimp, mussels, crawdads—I've even seen it catch the wing of a stray shorebird. If it can be caught, it will be eaten, feathers and all.

A stunned fish, soon to be a meal.

Filis' tentacles are covered in a sticky substance containing a mild, stinging sedative akin to that of an anemone, which renders its victims defenceless. Once caught, the mermaid pulls in its prey like a fisherman. With its mandibles it crushes the prey's skull, spine, or (if it is small) entire body. Usually this kills the prey instantly. It is lucky for us that *filis* measures only a few centimetres in length and is of little danger to humans.

To observe the hunting abilities of *filis* and find a medicinal use for the sedative component of its secretion, I temporarily removed some individuals from the coral reefs they inhabit to my laboratories. While I did my best to appropriately care for my charges and released them back into the wild after only a few weeks—a blip in the generally long lifespan of mermaids—a video of my activities has found its way online.

While I do love to share my discoveries with the world, uncontrolled leaks can have dire consequences. People were rightfully amazed by what they saw, yet their enthusiasm has led to increasing cases of *filis* being kept in home aquariums, where it can be easily observed and its gruesome skills can be turned into viral videos, clicks, and ad revenue. This is, of course, not legal and a real danger to both the individual creatures and the entire species, as mermaids are notoriously difficult to keep in an artificial environment. Yet it is a sad truth: Where there is a demand, there is a market, rendering even the fiercest predators powerless.

⚘ GORGÓNA ⚘
Gorgóna

The seas snakes that inhabit *Gorgóna gorgóna*'s head are a flurry of activity as they slither in knots and tangles. When studying them, I expected to hear the noise of rustling or hissing, but the perfect silence of the water envelops everything. It is strange to share space with a creature seemingly straight from Ovid's *Metamorphoses*, yet it is hard not to jump to this conclusion while observing the writhing mass of *Gorgóna gorgóna*'s hair. Elegant serpents wind around its head, their eyes open and alert. Of course, the elegant snakes do not grow directly from *gorgóna*'s scalp, even if it is where they nest and grew.

The symbiotic relationship begins with the adult mermaid shifting a clutch of snake eggs from its own or another *gorgóna*'s head onto that of its young once they reach roughly three years of age (by my calculations). The adult waits for the snakes to hatch and then, to encourage the snakes to remain with the young mermaid, it feeds them with shreds of fish, the young mermaid's blood, and its own milk, so the snakes become dependent on their new habitat. Eventually, the young mermaid takes over the care of the snakes, who in turn learn to take care of their habitat: the young mermaid.

Throughout their lives, the mermaid and the snakes share prey and predators alike. With uncountable sets of eyes, the *gorgóna* is a difficult mermaid to catch unawares and, with the assistance of multiple snakes, it proves a good hunter as well. All creatures, the mermaid and the snakes, feed on the spoils of their hunts and defend the mermaid's life whenever necessary, even if it requires the snakes to leave the safety of their home, something they do only with great reluctance, especially once they start to lay eggs.

Common sea snake.

I wondered at the many scars and marks on the *gorgóna*'s face and body and eventually came to understand that when food is scarce, both mermaid and snakes feed on each other, bite for bite, until a new source of nourishment is acquired, and the population can be sustained again. Older mermaids tend to display scarring in the facial and shoulder areas, while individuals that I surmise have gone through extended periods of hunger can be recognized by missing chunks of flesh down their torso and tail, their faces badly maimed.

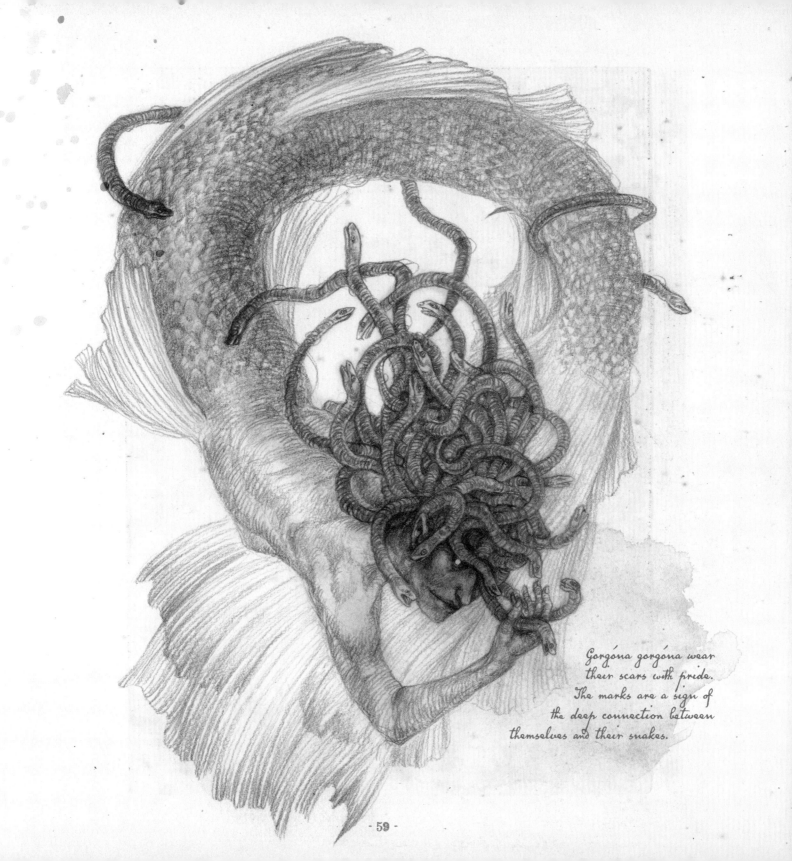

Gorgóna gorgóna wear
their scars with pride.
The marks are a sign of
the deep connection between
themselves and their snakes.

SEDNA
Inanis

Some mermaids are stranger than others. *Sedna inanis* is, in aesthetic, the very anthropocentric idea of mermaid; however, its activities and feeding habits are, for lack of a better word, otherworldly. As a scientist, there is little space for the metaphysical in my understanding of the world. Yet with these creatures, the paths of what is known to be true and what our human ancestors once believed to be true are crossing more often than I am comfortable with.

Inanis collects bladders from its victims. Did this mermaid play a role in inspiring any of the myths of the anirniq?

For decades, sightings of this mermaid have been reported near the coasts of Greenland and Canada. None of them were taken seriously. However, in light of new evidence, I can say that myth is also reality.

Inanis is an elusive creature that hunts the dying and the ill who seek out the ocean as an end to their life. The Inuit believe in anirniq: breath. All creatures have one breath that is part of a larger life force. It can be stolen and corrupted, which appears as sickness or death. Though I cannot claim to know what motivations drive this creature aside from satiation, I cannot help but wonder whether there is something more it seeks.

I have video material of *inanis* trailing an ailing narwhal near the end of its life. Upon catching up to the sinking narwhal, *inanis* did not devour it immediately but clutched it in what looked like a tight embrace until I noticed its long fingers digging into the pale flesh of its victim. While tearing up the narwhal's insides, *inanis'* mouth opened wide, and even through the silent recording, I could sense its heart-rending scream.

A later examination of the narwhal's corpse confirmed *inanis* had taken no more than its bladder. Is it *inanis* who inspired the belief of anirniq being stored in this organ? It is more likely that the narwhal's bladder contains specific nutrients *inanis* requires to subsist, even though we generally consider other organs healthier options. Or—and I hardly dare print this idea—is it the breath that *inanis* is feeding on? Down in the cold depths of the ocean a creature would need more nutrition than a bladder could provide.

SIRENA
Jenny Haniver

Even scientists get sick sometimes. After weeks and months of travelling the world in search of *Sirena*, I intended to return home for a quiet weekend and, of course, promptly fell ill. It is quite miserable to be around me in such a state, and my potted plants were lucky they had already dried up before my arrival and subsequent suffering. Besides the torment of fever and headaches, I was also afflicted with a ghastly insomnia that denied me much-needed sleep and had me roaming my empty apartment howling and bumping against furniture like a mortally wounded tiger. Delirium and fatigue tinted the mundane white walls in mystery, so it was little surprise that the memorabilia and curiosities I had gathered throughout the years took on a life of their own.

The same cruel power that kept my fragile body awake had forced the inanimate to join me in my endless wakefulness, and it seemed they were greater masters of their senses than I. The heart of my collection, a *Jenny Haniver* acquired during my time as a student in Antwerp, floated towards me and I remember it speaking to me. Though I cannot pull the words from my memory, the moment has stuck fast in my mind, and I shall not forget it. There is more to these creatures, the *Sirena*, than humanity can guess. Theirs is a world potentially full of culture and depth that we can only grasp at with our limited ability to accept other intelligences.

Jenny Haniver can appear in many different shapes and forms.

A few days after I had recovered, I received a phone call and realized that—consumed by manic fever—I must have sent a DNA sample of my *Jenny Haniver* to the lab. I had long assumed the *Jenny Haniver* to be a dried, carved, and physically manipulated fish (likely a skate). However, instead of having to apologize for wasted resources, I was asked to bring in the whole specimen for further investigation.

Now my lab has identified seven *Jenny Haniver*s as having mermaid DNA, allowing me to declare them a distinct species. I am working on a paper for publication discussing these fascinating creatures. If you own a *Jenny Haniver* specimen (which you may think is just a trinket or souvenir), please send it in for testing. Maybe you, too, have had a mermaid hiding in your home all along . . .

This is how my
Jenny Hanwer
appeared to me.

A view of this
creature from below.
What a marvelous
decoy!

SERRA
Picturae

My first documentation of this creature painted a very different mermaid, as I had not understood or perceived the creature correctly. Initially I placed its eyes where its nose is, but upon revisiting, I was forced to correct myself. Despite my strides within the world of sirenology, there are times when even I have to admit that my own studies are preliminary and far from perfect. Since my colleagues are a good-natured bunch, they only made fun of me for a few months and now only remind me of my error whenever they need to win an argument. (Archibald, of course, uses each and every one of my mistakes to discredit my entire body of work.)

A sketch to show what this remarkable creature looks like from the side.

Serra picturae's life and existence, of course, does not revolve around my professional ignominy. This mermaid has a giant nose, shaped like a humanoid face, to both smell and to confuse. Is it any wonder I mistook its nostrils for eyes?

My mistake was entirely by nature's design. *Picturae*'s nose ends in pointy horn-like protrusions, which are hard and pliable like bone, akin to the tooth of a narwhal. These horns are used to break through ice, coral, or sedimentary rock formations, in addition to hunting. This mermaid's eyes, its actual eyes, are rather large for its body; they are dome-shaped, like teacups, and they have an abundance of rods for light detection. Even in darkness, *picturae* has excellent vision. When *picturae* opens its mouth, the entirety of its upper face falls backwards, like a lid on a hinge. It looks like the wide slit of a maw tearing open its chest. This is fascinating and more than slightly disturbing to witness.

SERRA
Sphyrna

Serra sphyrna resides in the Indian Ocean and despite its impressive size—it is as heavy as a well-fed plough horse—this mermaid is surprisingly elusive if one does not know exactly where to look. *Sphyrna* lives on a diet of seagrass and skates, which regularly drives it into the open where a glimpse can be caught of this fast and nimble swimmer. Once sated, *sphyrna* returns to its hideaway in caves and burrows, safe from curious eyes and teeth. Due to the lack of hunting opportunities within *sphyrna*'s preferred domain, its cheek pouches are capable of extending up to three times their usual size and can store food that will last this mermaid up to a week.

Much of *sphyrna*'s life is spent in the darkness of caves, hence it has weak eyesight. Instead, this mermaid relies on its sense of smell and the ability to perceive small vibrations in the surrounding water, which is attributed to sensory organs located on the sides of its head.

While showing no hostility towards unrelated species, *sphyrna* does not favour the company of its own kin. Reproducing asexually, this mermaid bears a litter of up to ten pups during a five-year cycle. The parent cares for its young for about a month, during which the offspring generally reduce their own number by half out of territorial aggression and hunger. Because of their territorial nature, meetings between adult mermaids often end in blood.

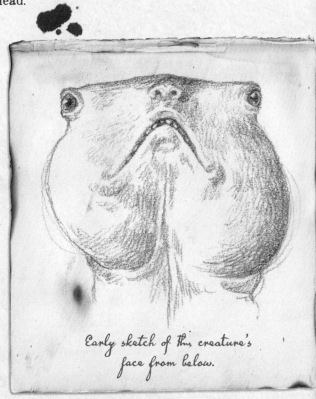

Early sketch of this creature's face from below.

Their shrinking habitat has brought this creature out into the open ocean more than usual and has also instigated brutal fights for the few burrows available. Scarcity of territory that can shield *sphyrna* from harm has led to a new development in the population. The strongest specimens remain true to the species' characteristic behaviour and hide away. Yet there have been accounts of young mermaids living together and swimming in the open, overcoming their natural instincts of slaughter and secrecy in favour of safety in community. The pups born into such groups often exhibit less aggressive traits, possibly influenced by the parent's closeness to other individuals' hormones during pregnancy.

Sphyrna is an
impressive oceanic figure
that is easily mistaken for
a hammerhead shark by locals
and tourists alike.

I suspect teuthida's ink glands may be located in the armpits.

SERRA
Teuthida

Serra teuthida (so far) reigns alone in the waters leading from the Pacific into the Sea of Japan. While this habitat is rich in flora and fauna due to the high amount of oxygen dissolved in the water, only one of these mermaids has made a home here, lurking where it is dark and quiet. As most mermaids do, *teuthida* reproduces asexually and very infrequently. It is only near the end of life that *teuthida* enters pregnancy and parenthood in silent solitude. Therefore, two grown specimens interacting has rarely been documented, and I have not witnessed it myself.

An adolescent Serra teuthida.

I imagine that, like other mermaids with similar behaviours, even if they may exhibit initial curiosity, they are ultimately territorial and cannot cohabitate unless under extreme environmental or predatory duress. If it were not to satiate hunger, *teuthida* would never rise and interact with the world and its myriad creatures.

I posit it is likely this mermaid has poor eyesight, and so what it can see when it rises is questionable. It doesn't display any use of sight, rather the opposite. It emits ink that blots out the light and confuses the senses of the fish and crustaceans that become *teuthida*'s meal.

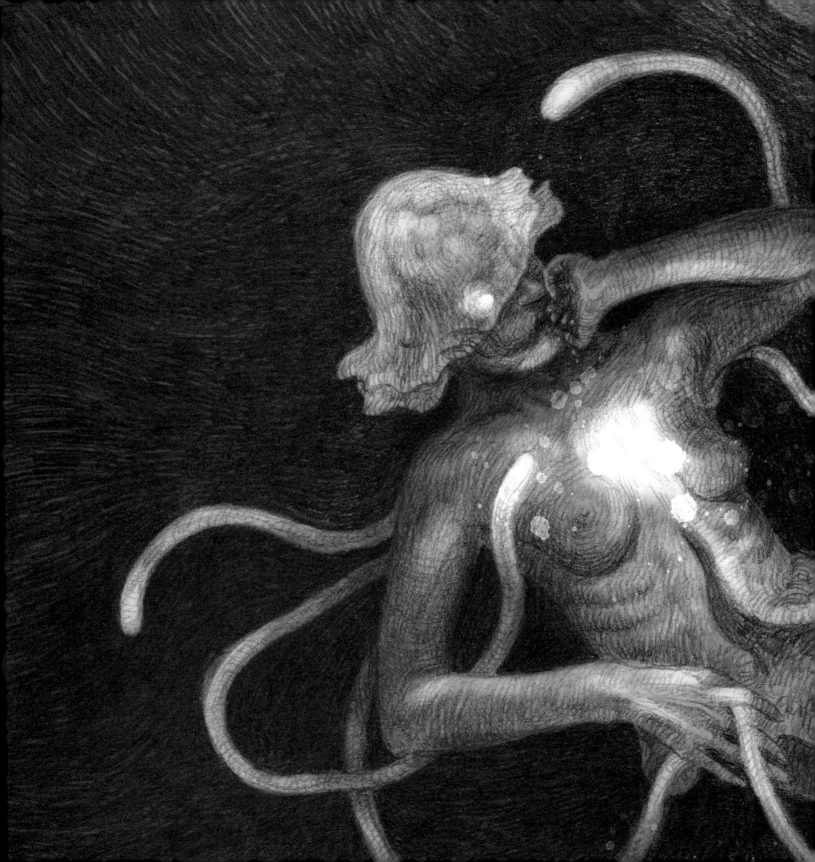

SERRA
Cinereo.

Deep down within the volcanic structures located in the South Atlantic, a single mermaid dwells and hides, patiently waiting for prey to swim into its open palms. *Serra cinereo* looks like a sculpture, obsidian traversed by rivulets of gold, and like a sculpture, it is poised and unmoving. It is so still that algae will settle and grow upon it, and following the algae are its prey: fish. A curious or hungry fish suddenly, inexplicably, found itself in the grasp of a mermaid. This creature is so nimble and its movement so restrained, I barely noticed that it had gone from a statue with palms open to a statue gently clutching a fish which, in a graceful vanishing act, then disappeared into its maw. For one short moment *cinereo*'s jaw gaped open, wide enough to swallow the entire fish. Its lines of razor-sharp teeth suggest larger prey is part of this mermaid's diet, if only quick bites out of passing whales or sharks. Of the small fish, not even a scale was left behind, and *cinereo* quickly settled back into its accustomed position, resting and waiting for its next catch.

I imagine cinereo belonging to a long-lost temple like this.

With its perfectly humanoid features, *cinereo* looks like a statue made for worship in a temple, but if there ever was such a structure, it has long since fallen apart. Indeed, its home region was completely void of humanity until the discovery of the Saint Helena territory in the sixteenth century. Even today, the area is far richer in birds than it is in people. Unless *cinereo* originated elsewhere, perhaps a remnant of the many ships wrecked in these waters, there must once have been more of its kind inhabiting the region. What culture and society could have been lost to the sand and sea? A few hopeful archaeologists and anthropologists have joined my studies, excited for yet another forgotten culture to be discovered, even whispering about the fabled Atlantis. Yet all there is to guide us is this solitary creature, a mermaid with a talent for melting into the shadows and becoming as insubstantial as the phantom city itself.

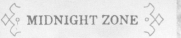
SERRA

Cursor Manibus

This incredible creature boasts five limbs and ink-secreting glands along the ridges of its fins. The slow, controlled movements of its dorsal and caudal fins distribute the substance evenly. A cloud of darkness spreads, which allows *Serra cursor manibus* to escape any danger, or unwanted study, with ease. *Cursor manibus* is fast when necessary, accelerating with a powerful tail and using its webbed extremities to race along the sand.

Cursor manibus holds onto the sea floor with a light touch; only friction keeps it grounded. When hunting, it moves on all fours along the bottom of the shallow sea, the sand sliding smoothly between its dactyls, barely kicking up clouds. After extensive observation, I can now posit that these mermaids have an uncanny sensitivity to vibrations in the ground. *Cursor manibus* can root out the tiniest creature, the mere inkling of fish eggs buried and hidden. With the sensitivity of its hands and feet comes a preference for soft meals, often near invisible to the human eye, such as the larvae of mussels. However, *cursor manibus* occasionally goes after larger prey like sea slugs. With its quick, almost supernatural perception and protective ink, this mermaid does not need to worry much about predation itself, ensuring a reasonably well-fed and carefree existence.

A portrait sketch. While I was studying this creature it seemed to study me right back.

Front claws

Hind claws

Note the sturdier hind claws

Cursor manibus is a strange
but captivating sight, and
though its many limbs look
cumbersome this mermaid
is actually quite quick.

Exciting news!
During the editing of this manuscript,
a field agent called to let me know
decipula has closed its mouth,
swallowing the
ecosystem whole.

It remains to be
seen when decipula
will decide to reopen
the gates to its honey trap.

⚓ SIRENA ⚓
Decipula

A strange oasis lies deep down where life is scarce and light is scant. Here come the lost and the out of place, stumbling upon a small island of warmth and nutrients far away from home. Here aquatic plants, corals, and sea anemones rarely seen elsewhere can be found, and from them spawn sea life unique to this little ecosystem. Even with my trained eyes and guided by a colleague's instructions, it took me half an hour to scour the darkness for this wonderfully prosperous place. The cave hosts guests ranging from tiny polyps to small sharks and seems miraculous until the curve of a cheek, the dark hollows of nostrils, and a pair of unblinking eyes become apparent in the light of my torch. *Sirena decipula* lies asleep with its body hidden deep in the earth, skin calcified, mouth wide open. This is where fish play in the fluorescent light of strange seagrass, where crustaceans climb over mossy mussels. It is paradise.

A sketch of what the whole specimen would look like.

Decipula is not a bivalve like a clam; instead, I strongly suggest it is of the *Sirena* family and, as indicated by my sketch, that its body is indeed buried. It has not always been here, yet I doubt it could still move its position, as it is encased by the geology of the sea floor. I wonder how long it has been resting in this spot? I am curious to see how the shifting of the earth's crust might affect this creature. Would it be shaken free so that it could once again migrate or would it be destroyed? These are just some of the questions I have about this mermaid. Does it have cognitive abilities similar to our species and is it capable of planning, of cunning and trickery? Or does it merely react to its surroundings? I dare not anthropomorphize these creatures too much, but it is difficult not to wonder about the Sirena as so many of them have features much like our own.

Decipula's gaping mouth offers a one-of-a-kind haven, only to feed on those who enter like its very own vegetable garden. Again and again and again. Creation and destruction everlasting. I will return to this creature, watch it open up, chart the growth of the flora and fauna, record any possible movements of the *decipula,* and hopefully witness the end of the next cycle myself.

SERRA
Hortus.

When the corpse of a whale sinks to the bottom of the ocean it creates its own unique ecosystem called a whale fall. Decay is slow in the cold depths of the oceanic abyss, and the giant carcass offers food and refuge to all manner of ocean life. Decades can pass before this oasis of life in death is finally consumed or buried. *Serra hortus* emulates this.

A portrait of the Dreamer.

How old is this creature and what has it thought of throughout its ages?

I find myself wondering how humankind has affected this creature, if at all, and whether its demise will be due to our destructive force.

Hortus has become a garden lying still and overgrown on the ocean floor. For a human, it is nearly impossible to imagine a stationary existence, to have critters tunnelling through your flesh, roots mingling with your veins, and an entire ecosystem depending on you. In return, as flora and fauna live and die their corpses become sustenance for the rest of the ecosystem, including *hortus* itself. In fact, I have the suspicion this mermaid can, with enough time and nutrition, regrow vital parts of its body. However, once *hortus* finally passes away, like when a whale fall is entirely consumed, all the creatures that were sustained by it will pass too.

How long can *hortus* sustain this tiny universe, replenishing itself while nourishing corals and bacteria, crustaceans, fish, and sea anemones? None of the species alive in and on *hortus* can be found anywhere else in the world. This mermaid has lived through prehuman times, long enough to allow the species who are now part of its body to develop into something genetically different from their ancestors. This mermaid is old enough to have seen evolution take place on its very back—and it has done it all in absolute stillness. In my mind, I have come to call *hortus* "The Dreamer," unable to keep myself from anthropomorphizing this creature. It has a functioning brain, but is it conscious? What is it thinking about? Is it in a meditative state? It is a romantic notion belonging only to this journal, but to me, it is a beautiful thought that a creature could *willingly* exist in an eternal partnership with an ecosystem like this. Alas, I will never know the true will and intent of this creature, but I can still dream that one day humanity will truly embrace the grand ecosystem that is planet Earth.

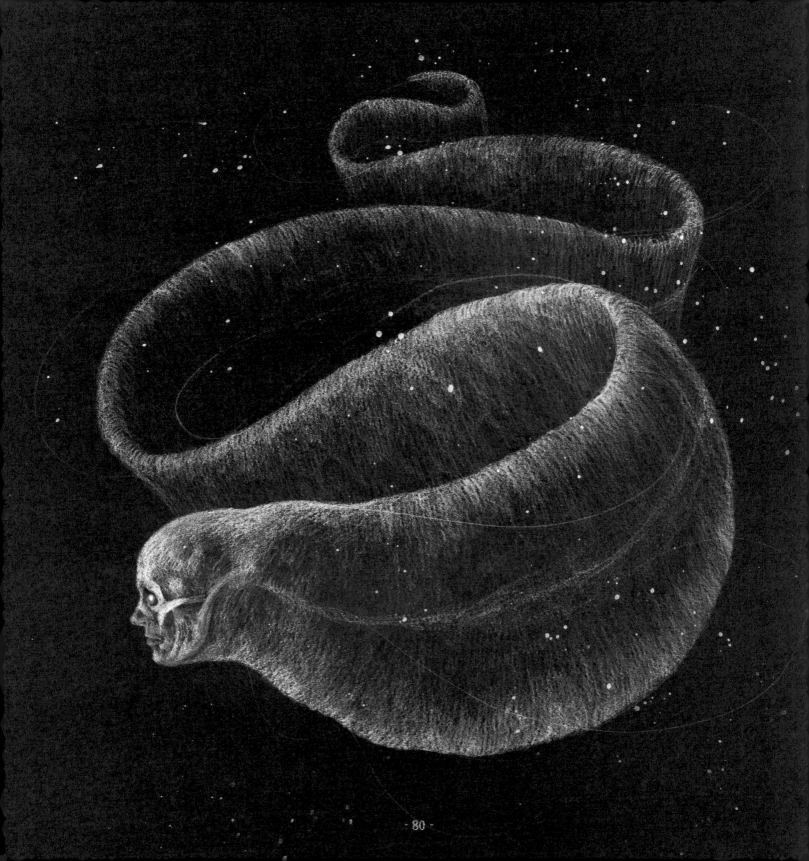

SERRA

Leptocephalus

Drifting aimlessly along deep-sea currents, *Serra leptocephalus* sustains itself solely on the gelatinous material stored in its own body. Besides the cranium, there is no visible skeleton; what exists of a nervous system is negligible. *Leptocephalus'* soft inner mass is wrapped in only a thin layer of muscle and skin, lending it both shape and movement.

While this does answer the general questions of subsistence and environment, no sirenologist worth their salt would find their curiosity quenched without learning how this mermaid's body is created and what happens once its store of sustenance is exhausted. Fortunately, these questions can now be answered due to recent observations, even if not entirely to my satisfaction. With only its head and a fraction of what I call its "frame" left, the muscle formerly holding the mermaid together disintegrates, and the mucus of its innards slowly oozes out. The shape it takes throughout this gestation period resembles a foggy cloud hovering around *leptocephalus'* head. With time, small particles of minerals and plankton catch onto the sticky surface, slowly building up body mass again. When enough matter has accumulated (approximately 1m³ in volume), the head is restored to its outward position while muscle and nerves are regrown. To the human eye, the whole process seems glacial, spanning up to a decade. One wonders whether or perhaps how the few months of conscious, self-consuming existence that follow are worth the effort.

When all that remains constant is a head (skull and brain matter) what are the complex thoughts and feelings of this creature?

Minerals and plankton.

❧ SERRA ❧
Macrourida

Birth is a dangerous business. The comfort of modern medicine has made this easy for many of us to forget. Yet maternal mortality is still a force to be reckoned with in nature. In every creation of a new life, death is faced and hopefully evaded. *Serra macrourida*, however, opts for the reassurance of certainty and embraces death instead.

This Arctic, deep-sea mermaid lives a long life, full of ferocity and carnage. There are no tricks to its hunting, only teeth and claws and will. Considering its low reproduction rate, such a life seems careless, a danger to the survival of the species, for which every individual is precious. It is unknown to me whether this mermaid is aware of the ending the first swelling of its body heralds, how it forebodes the bloating of decay that will soon reshape it.

I also do not know if *macrourida* can choose when pregnancy begins, as with all asexually reproducing creatures one cannot simply point to insemination as the cause. What ultimately sets off that slow poison? Is it age, weakness, illness? Perhaps it is an environmental factor, a change in temperature or a decrease in predators. Whatever the cause, a *macrourida*'s natural life cycle begins and ends with death. While studying these creatures, I found myself wondering if in the end the mermaid felt fear or anger at the inevitable, or whether it was consumed by love for the future offspring. Does this creature live in blissful, violent ignorance until one day its belly tears open and it sees its own juvenile face staring back at it? Does *macrourida* remember its own birth and the weeks of sheltering in its mother's remains until strong enough to fend for itself? Does it make peace with its own end, knowing it will now provide life and safety for its kin? But these are anthropocentric wonderings of my own. It is likely *macrourida*'s experience is beyond my human capacity to understand.

A young macrourida peers out at me from a sea cave.

An adult macrourida hunting for prey—living its life well and in good health, it prepares itself for the next generation whether it knows it or not.

I eventually caught a snapshot of pellucidum existing where no human can. What a beautiful and alien creature.

SERRA
Pellucidum

For weeks it seemed like the promise of frostbite was the only thing Antarctica had to offer. As with love, loss, and life, it was when I had nearly called off the search that the mermaid finally surfaced. *Serra pellucidum* is close to completely transparent, and therefore nearly invisible in the pitch black of the ocean. This mermaid has a crystalline body and is adept at preserving energy. Even its circulatory system has adapted to the cold. Its blood lacks red cells, which makes it easier to pump through its veins. The reduced ability to transport oxygen matters little since the water of the southern deep sea is incredibly rich with it. In other waters, *pellucidum* would not be able to survive, effectively limiting its habitat.

Ice fish blood shares the same properties as that of pellucidum.

As a member of a species that has made a point of invading every part of the Earth, *pellucidum*'s confinement seems to be ours as well. This mermaid may never see a green coastline, but neither are humans ever likely to fully explore and understand the dark depths of the ocean. I wonder what this creature sees down there, what mysteries exist beyond human reach. Again, I remind myself this creature likely has a mind wired entirely differently from my own and it is fascinating to consider how it might perceive the world, whether changes in the water pressure, temperature, or chemical make-up affect what it sees or how it communicates. What does *pellucidum* see where we perceive only emptiness?

Pellucidum is as translucent as the Antarctic ice floating in the frigid ocean.

✠ PHENOMENON ✠
Reanimatus·

If we talk about life after death, we rarely include our earthly bodies in the concept, and if we do, we prefer to think about the new life that is begotten from them; the flowers growing once the flesh has decomposed; rather than of corpses rotting in graves. It would be uncomfortable to think of the worms, insects, and microbes doing their crucial work. Yet for mermaids this is the only time during which *reanimatus* occurs.

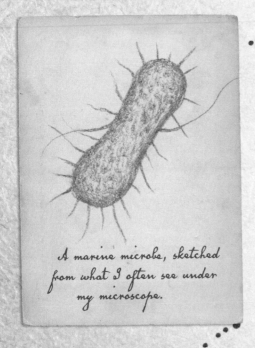

A marine microbe, sketched from what I often see under my microscope.

We all carry invisible passengers with us. Around two per cent of our bodyweight consists of bacteria, primarily in our gastrointestinal tract. After we die, they continue to digest food for us, and once that is gone, they consume us from the inside.

Mermaids (at least the ones I've examined) tend to house a similar amount of microbes to humans, if not more. *Reanimatus* is what happens if the microbes in a mermaid that has died travel into its brain and muscles to pull the strings for a while instead of feasting quietly on its organs. While *reanimatus* is far clumsier than a living mermaid (and thus quickly identified by its awkward movements), the body continues to follow many of the living mermaid's behaviours, including the consumption of food. This consumption may be the reason this phenomenon happens (or at least lasts long enough to be observed by a sirenologist) primarily in herbivore species, as the harvesting of plants and algae requires less dexterity than the hunting of prey.

How exactly this phenomenon comes to be and whether any vestiges of consciousness of the mermaid remain during *reanimatus* are still mysteries to be solved. Indeed, the existence of both *reanimatus* and *caeruleus* as death-related phenomena is puzzling, especially as the latter leaves no body to animate behind. Is *reanimatus* proof of *caeruleus* not being an occurrence in all mermaid species or of it happening only under specific circumstances? Or perhaps *reanimatus* is what happens if the process of *caeruleus* cannot be completed due to a sudden and unexpected death? Perhaps the mermaid's microbiome simply does not realize its task is done until the body has fallen apart. Or does it enjoy its new prospective life as a mammal? Even though *reanimatus* slows down the decay of the body, it ultimately cannot stop it. Eventually the mermaid's second life ends, and nature takes its course.

SERRA

Synanceia

One creature's nectar is another's poison. As aquatic plants creep up *Serra synanceia*'s body, feeding on the thick film of goo covering its shell from tail to torso, any fish taking a tentative bite succumbs to its potent neurotoxin. They are paralysed, if not dead, on the spot. Where flora thrives, fauna dies, and *synanceia* feeds on both.

This mermaid lives a quiet life compared to some of its more active cousins. Like *Sirena decipula* or *Serra hortus*, it leads an existence much like a rock. Unlike these other mermaids, however, *synanceia* does move slowly, like a snail beneath an oversized shell. *Synanceia* is not eroded from but rather added to by time and the elements. Every grain of sand, every splinter of stone caught in the substance *synanceia* secretes stays preserved like brick in mortar, creating camouflage and providing a fertile ground for seaweeds and other ocean flora with shallow roots.

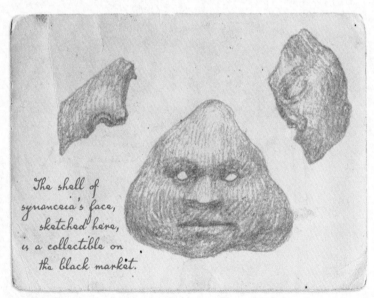

The shell of synanceia's face, sketched here, is a collectible on the black market.

Beneath the layer of debris lies *synanceia*'s shell. The material is just dense enough to weigh the mermaid to the sea floor without hindering *synanceia*'s slow, subtle movements. It is difficult for it to swim, enveloped by its shell, but luckily this is unnecessary. Faced with danger, *synanceia* hides almost completely inside its shell, leaving nothing but poisonous, hard skin exposed. It is almost impossible to harm *synanceia* and most predators do not even try, treating it as a rock formation, however peculiar it may be. After *synanceia* dies, time and tiny creatures hollow out its shell, which soon becomes a place of refuge for fish and smaller mermaids, as the poison fades from the wild garden growing on the outer hull.

SIRENA Velum

The intrigue of a veil is undeniable. *Sirena velum's* reveals only the hint of eyes and a mouth, but what truly hides underneath are venomous fangs and milky, false eyes. Indeed I posit this creature has no functional eyes but rather reads its environment through temperature shifts and movement. The photophores dangling from *velum's* face and body glow bright in the dark of the deep sea and look like a curtain of dancing lights. The fish they attract are caught unawares by the jaws hiding behind. Indeed, perhaps I'll add *mortis* to this creature's name, for truly it is a veil of death. Still, there are worse ways to die, as this mermaid's teeth are very sharp.

Velum undertakes a—and I have no other words for it—ritual, or maybe custom, with its victims. *Velum* devours any flesh its prey offers, then rips out the bones, licks them clean, and pierces itself with them. While I, a human, may be reminded of jewellery underlining this ferocious appearance, these added spikes might serve as a sort of armour as well. Then again, there isn't much in the deep sea that threatens *velum*, which leads me to wonder what other practical or specialized *Sirena* use this could serve. Even if Archibald and his sycophants will sniff at the notion, I cannot but consider it a memorial ritual, perhaps to honour the lives lost to enable *velum's* own. It might also be a proud, macabre display of its hunting merit. Either way, I believe it proves a depth of thought and feeling science is traditionally reluctant to attest to non-*Homo* species. Naturally, further study is needed in order to find a conclusive explanation for this habit, but I will need updated deep-sea equipment to do so.

Like a creature from a horror movie, emerging from the dark, deep waters.

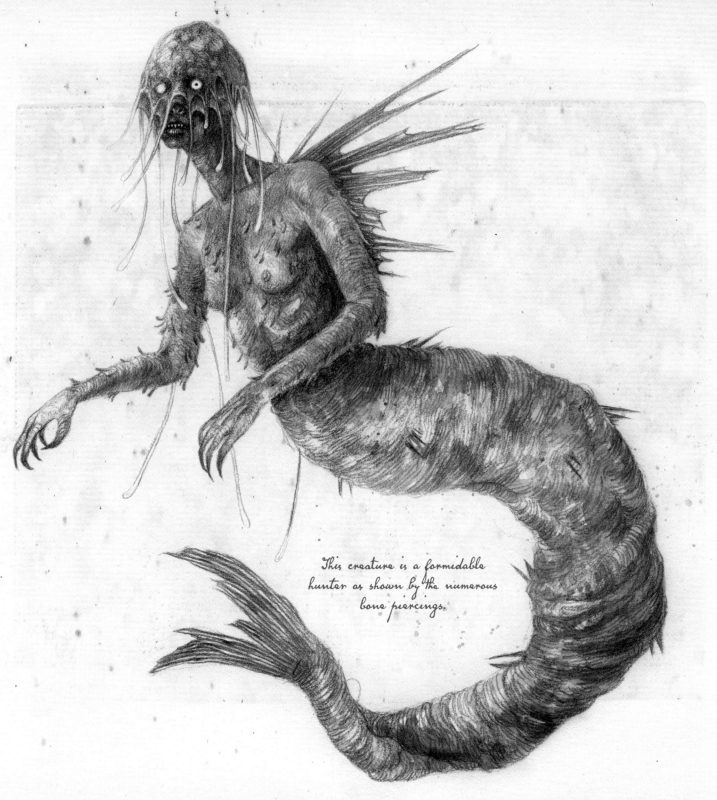

This creature is a formidable
hunter as shown by the numerous
bone piercings.

SERRA
Visum

Serra *visum* has two mouths. Though perhaps not the most interesting of this specimen's characteristics, it is the most noticeable. If *visum* is observed in its natural habitat, its lower mouth is not so easily spotted, buried as it is on the ocean floor. *Visum* covers its whole body with sand using big, webbed, shovel-like limbs. Once buried, only the spikes on its back and upper face remain visible, blinking skywards.

This creature's camouflage is so effective that the chances of a human passer-by spotting it are nearly impossible. Only when small fish swim into its spikes, mistaking them for a row of seagrass, can movement be seen as the fish, losing focus, begins to drift dazed and confused. *Visum* then lifts its head and opens its upper mouth, a fleshy cavity in its occiput, to eat the unfortunate fish. A short time later, I witnessed the maw below chewing and swallowing as the food presumably travelled down an inner passage connecting the two mouths. The lower mouth has no teeth, but barbules specialized in sifting through the sea floor for plankton and small crustaceans. In addition to this creature's fascinating features, it is also the only mermaid known to be capable of producing electrical charges, which it uses to stun its prey like the unlucky fish mentioned above.

Front view

Side view

I am excited to report that a specimen of *visum* is on its way to the lab! I look forward to autopsying this creature to get a better understanding of how its two mouths work, what its inner digestive system looks like, and how the electrical current is produced naturally.

Visum's spikes electrocuting its prey.

Visum is fascinating because its camouflage seems to be from both marine animals and humans alike.

Lake Zone

FRESHWATER MERMAIDS & PHENOMENA

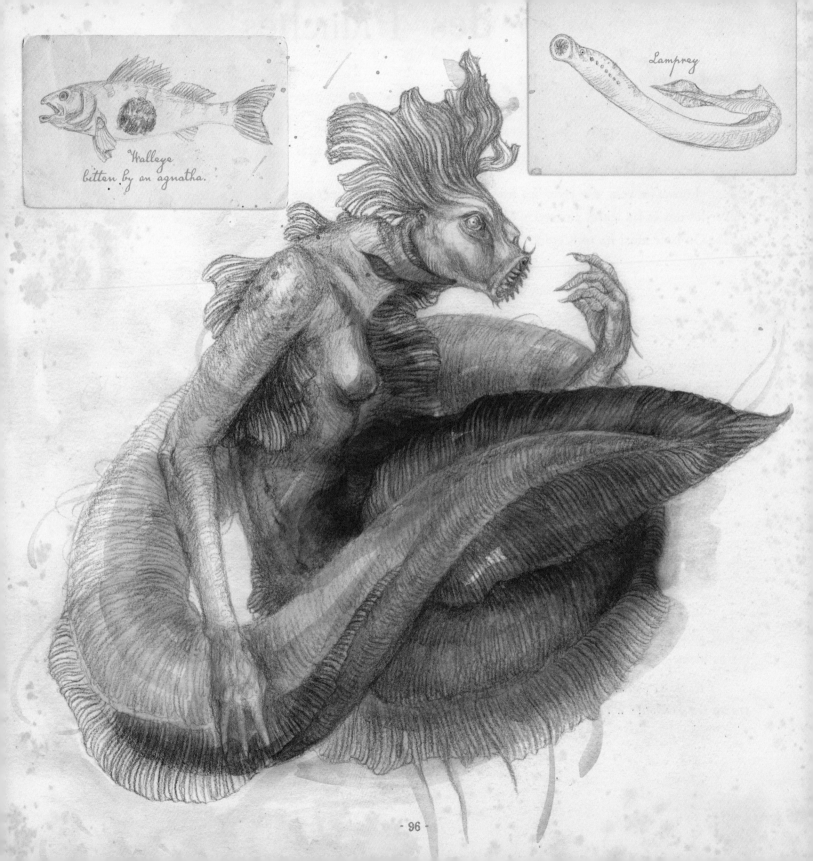

Walleye
bitten by an agnatha.

Lamprey

◆ SIRENA ◆
Agnatha

The world is small, and when broken into fields of acumen and study, it shrinks even further. The study of this mermaid would have been impossible without like-minded colleagues. I was following a trail brought to me by a fellow researcher in Canada who had noticed peculiar deaths in the walleye population of Lake Erie. Every now and then, one of the large, golden fish was found drained of blood and with a gaping hole in its side. The attacker didn't seem to possess a jaw, carving as much as sucking pieces from their prey. Most were considering an overachieving lamprey as the culprit; however, my friend knew of my particular interest in strange aquatic creatures and was wise to call me. Unfortunately, even after months of observation and the strategic installation of underwater cameras, I found nothing but more dead walleyes.

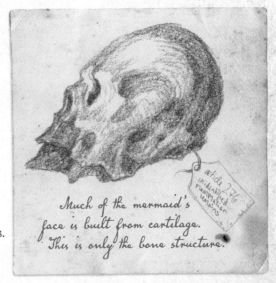

Much of the mermaid's face is built from cartilage. This is only the bone structure.

Then I received a parcel from an Austrian colleague. Inside was a skull with a tale attached:

Once upon a time, a river meandered through the gentle slope of the idyllic countryside of Austria. In it, there lived a mermaid. She lived, she thrived, and as the world shifted and changed, she died. Her body became one with the riverbed, and when the water evaporated, it revealed her naked bones to the world. Time covered her with a blanket of heavy soil and planted a grove of wildflowers on the grave of the river. When humans came, they burnt the nettles and tore up the earth to build their homes of cement and steel, and she was unearthed. A man took the fossil of her skull and put it on a shelf and then into a box where she hid for nearly two decades, growing a skin of dust in the dark.

It was my turn to try my hand at prying answers from this specimen. My first instinct was to travel to Austria at once, to leave my dead end in Ontario for greener pastures. However, the freshwater river this creature used to swim in existed no more, and I knew it.

Oh, I was ready to throw that precious skull into Lake Erie, dead end to dead end, when it struck me! My *agnatha* was not incomplete or damaged but was a jawless creature, just like the murderous mermaids I was currently chasing. Perhaps it was an ancestor or even *agnatha* itself. This is, of course, mere speculation until I finally find this elusive creature, yet the idea has invigorated my research.

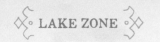
SERRA
Phoenicopterus

The alkaline lake where this mermaid resides is at once a magnificent and ghastly place, as illustrated by the calcified bodies of birds and other creatures who have found their end decorating the shore of these caustic waters. For *Serra phoenicopterus*, life in this inhospitable brew of chemicals is easy as there are no rivals or predators around. *Phoenicopterus* basks in waters as hot as forty degrees Celsius, the high temperatures and the caustic properties of the water harmless to its skin and scales. It feeds on the few lifeforms that can coexist in this environment, algae, bacteria, and tiny crabs, which it gulps down with a mouthful of mud.

In much the same way a flamingo takes on its classic pink colour, the crustacean- and algae-filled diet of this mermaid gives it a bright magenta colouration that contrasts with the liquid kelly green of the lake. While this environment can seem dead on the surface, it is a thriving ecosystem with a vividly coloured apex predator.

Bird's eye view of the alkaline lake where I discovered phoenicopterus.

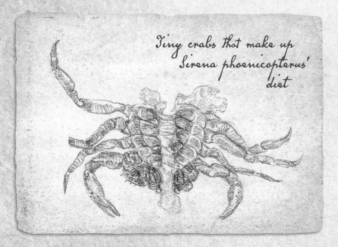

Tiny crabs that make up *Sirena phoenicopterus'* diet

Unfortunately, I could spend only a week with this creature, as my gear was damaged too severely by the water. However, I have already ordered specialized equipment and cannot wait to resume my observations! It must be a good life for *phoenicopterus*, though possibly lonely. Procreation and species survival for this specimen is a serious question: Does it spontaneously reproduce or is this one creature the last of its kind, unknowingly awaiting extinction?

SIRENA
Spinosa

I have witnessed this mermaid feeding on a wide array of mammals, ranging from rabbits to deer. *Sirena spinosa*, one of many adept hunters among the mermaids, is not averse to simply chasing prey down out in the open, but it has another weapon in its arsenal: the Siren Song. Our own recordings do not do this mermaid's voice justice, but in-the-flesh witness accounts describe following the luring call through dense forest thickets, only for the person to notice the scratches and torn clothes once they wake from their trance. Our ear witnesses were lucky *spinosa*'s caught something or somebody else before they arrived at its lair: an overgrown lake with crystal clear water. Once victims come near *spinosa*'s spiked tail, they are likely lost. The tail can pierce even the toughest animal hide, creating a deep puncture wound from which *spinosa* sucks its prey's blood.

Spinosa's "bloody kiss."

A close up of spinosa's tail and stinger.

While larger victims like stags or wild boars often survive an attack, smaller ones such as rabbits drown due to the weakness and disorientation caused by blood loss. After thorough investigation and establishing the mermaid's lack of killing intent, one of my colleagues decided to rid himself of his earplugs, planning on submitting himself to the mermaid in the name of science. Of course, I did my best to ensure his safety. I cannot lie, I was very eager to see what would happen and what he would have to report. Would it hurt? Was there a sedative in the mermaid's bloody kiss or was its song enough to keep its prey docile? Unfortunately, our questions were never answered. What was witnessed was a gruesome reminder not to draw direct conclusions from zoological studies for human use, as this mermaid clearly considered us a special treat.

SIRENA
Venis.

In 1875 volcanic eruptions broke open the surface of the Icelandic volcano Askja—which some academics posit is also the mythological Asgard—creating craters such as Viti (or "hell") and Öskjuvatn, a lake reaching 220 m in depth within which lives a mermaid. *Sirena venis* appears humanoid in many ways. In particular, *venis'* face and hair are those of a beautiful young woman, which truly reflects the legend of the mermaid.

The most remarkable part of *venis* is the bright green colour that shines through its near transparent skin, suggesting the presence of chloroplasts at a high percentage. The lake is covered in ice during the colder months of the year, locking *venis* in the murky depths to feed on algae and microorganisms. By the time summer frees the lake's surface of ice, its stores of chloroplasts have been replenished, allowing it to generate additional energy by photosynthesis. Yet certainly a complex organism like *venis* requires a greater variety of nutrients than water, sun, and sparse vegetation can offer? Perhaps it is possible this mermaid shares further similarities with plants or bacteria that I have not yet been able to discover.

Past disappearances by travellers from Öskjuvatn, *venis'* habitat, have been blamed on its potentially predatory nature. Such speculations are wholly unfounded, however, as there has yet to be any evidence of her aggression towards humans or other animals, let alone remains showing signs of a mermaid attack. It is more likely these people fell victim to the less cryptozoological dangers that come with exploring untamed nature: rockslides and inclement weather. Askja is, after all, an active volcano and its landscape is subject to ongoing change.

During the summer of 1902, two German scientists vanished without a trace while taking a boat trip on Öskjuvatn.

On some days the creature seems to be entirely absent, undoubtedly due to *venis'* ingenuity when it comes to discovering hideouts. Yet once you leave the more sophisticated realm of sirenology, there are whispers of hidden portals and pathways to a world more wondrous than our own, used by the sirens to escape the hustle and bustle of the Anthropocene. One can only hope for these to be true, as otherwise this shy mermaid may starve without the necessary boost of sunlight to revitalize it before the long winter under the ice.

Chloroplasts found on the surface of venis' skin.

Since the area has been made accessible by road, it has become busy with tourists during the summer, eager to marvel at the blue of Öskjuvatn and to take a swim in Víti's geothermal warmth.

This increase in activity seems to have spooked the mermaid, as sightings of venis soaking in sunlight during the warm months, which should be common, have become increasingly rare.

River Zone

FRESHWATER MERMAIDS & PHENOMENA

SERRA
Arapaima

In a time of myth and magic, the mightiest of the Amazonian gods, Tupã, conspired with his fellow gods against Pirarucu, who was the fiercest of warriors. He had become cruel and vain, so the gods brought on a thunderstorm to strike him with lightning. Wounded, Pirarucu fell into the wild waters of the Tocantins River, and there he turned into a large fish made from shadows, haunting the river ever since.

This old Amazonian legend does not mention whether he finally meets his equal in *Serra arapaima*, nor whether the mermaid *is* the transformed warrior himself. Despite being heavily armoured with tough scales, this mermaid, nearly four metres in length, is a fast and efficient swimmer.

Serra arapaima hunts birds by jumping out of the water to catch them midflight, then plunging back down to drown them.

While otherwise hard to spot in the countless murky rivers of the Amazon basin, *arapaima* can be observed when it breaks through the surface to breathe. While a solitary nature is common for mermaids, this species is openly hostile towards *any* living creature and shows no mercy when protecting its territory. It feeds on fish, crustaceans, small mammals, and sometimes birds. So far, no *arapaima* has been caught and no remains have been uncovered; however, fearful tales of its strong jaws have spread far.

Fishermen's tales are our strongest link to these creatures. *Arapaima* is very similar to the pirarucu fish, which is hunted for its meat and size; and thus, unlucky fishermen stalk the mermaid by accident. One notable account described an *arapaima* smashing a hole into the hull of a fishing boat, capsizing the small wooden vessel. Thankfully, the owner made it back to shore, if barely. Indeed, our observations show *arapaima* revels in the hunt, leaving the half-heartedly chewed remains of its prey adrift in its wake, already stealing after the next victim.

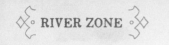

❧ SERRA ❧
Oblita

Most mermaids, like other large marine creatures, are uninterested in hunting and preying on humans; humans may be tricked or lured to their demise by a mermaid like *Sirena medusa clara*, but few hunt us in the way that *Serra oblita* does. *Oblita* is a freshwater dweller, at home in the rivers and marshes of the Indian subcontinent. Despite being an agile swimmer, this mermaid prefers the shallows, which allow it to wade onshore with its four tail fins, reinforced by bone and muscle like those of a walrus or sea lion. It is not particularly fast, and its scuttling gait may at first seem ridiculous, but there is little cause for laughter once this mermaid is close enough to lash out with its tail or bite.

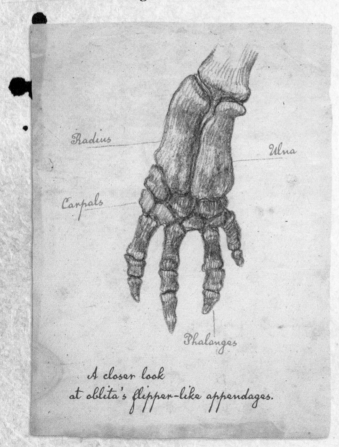

Radius

Ulna

Carpals

Phalanges

A closer look at oblita's flipper-like appendages.

Oblita generally prefers small spotted deer or wild goat to our gangly human limbs, but it will stalk and prey on humans—which in part can account for its rarity. There are only so many children that can disappear before humans, the apex predators on this planet, take reciprocal action. Before sirenologists had the time to become concerned about *oblita*'s conservation, the local human population made great efforts to secure their own survival and hunted or poached *oblita*'s numbers to near extinction. Now the species is so rare, it is nearly forgotten by all but sirenologists like me. *Oblita*'s kills are often attributed to crocodiles, who share its habitat.

I have been tracking down relics made from mermaid skin, bone, and leather estimated to be several hundreds of years old, and I have been collecting local folk tales to reconstruct an image of *oblita*. My efforts to spot a living individual have so far merely succeeded in the loss of one of my team members. I have decided to suspend the search indefinitely.

Oblita first came to me
through folklore and monster
stories, which are, of course,
nearly always grounded in truth.

As the mermaid is pulled along the river, it grows resilient. With its strong fingers and forearms it learns to dig into the riverbed and pebbles to keep itself steady even as the current relentlessly rushes on.

✷ SERRA ✷
Repere.

Serra repere's life starts as one of many hatchlings in a picturesque mountain lake. From cracks in the rocks below, fresh water feeds the lake until it spills over into a river. A juvenile mermaid knows well to stay clear of the currents that will take it on a journey along fast-flowing rapids and leisurely meanders, terminating in the sea. However, its home can only sustain one hive queen and her immediate court, so once *repere* has reached maturity, now the size of a sturdy twig, it is time to leave, starve, or die in territorial disputes.

Repere learns to read the river, knows when to let go and be transported to a new hunting ground, knows when a rapid will catapult it into the air to catch insects mid-flight. Sometimes such an attempt will leave *repere* stranded on land. Yet steeled as it is by the river, dragging itself back into the water poses no problem as long as it remains unhurt. Unfortunately, sometimes the landing will leave *repere* with broken bones or deep wounds. In this case, it is likely to perish quickly and be picked up by a hungry fox or curious sirenologist.

Serra repere catching a dragonfly mid-flight.

Of course, I will never know whether the mermaid is aware the river will eventually carry it to the sea, which for a pure freshwater creature can only end in death. Taking this into consideration, the *repere*'s struggle to stay in place may read like a struggle to prolong its very existence. Yet this is my sentimentality getting the better of me. *Repere* is not clinging to rocks and flinging itself through the air to ward off death any more than any other living creature. We are all driven to survive and thrive by instinct.

I would love to have a long-term study of *repere*'s population through the last centuries as many rivers were forced into unnatural shapes, destroying wetland ecosystems, which not only benefit *repere* but many creatures including us humans, as these areas naturally prevent the flooding of our dwellings. In a healthy ecosystem I imagine the number of mermaids being spilled out into the sea would be lower as more can find a home along the way. However, less new hives settling would also lead to a general decline of the population, leading to less mermaids for us to recover at the estuary mouth. Sometimes finding many dead simply means the population is thriving, sad as it may make me feel.

SERRA
Segmenta

*S*erra *segmenta's* numerous fins work constantly in perfect coordination with each other, so that it easily maneuvers in the rushing waters of the Congo River. While the river and its estuaries are this mermaid's primary habitat, it can also be found off the coast of Africa where the Congo River merges with the Atlantic Ocean, showing great adaptability to water salinity. Considering the extensive size of *segmenta*'s territory, I speculate this mermaid travels over ten thousand kilometers throughout its life.

Segmenta is quite large, dwarfed perhaps by *arapaima*, this mermaid is about two meters in length. I have only made visual contact with segmenta twice during my travels as, despite its impressive size, a sharp eye is needed to catch a glimpse of this mermaid: Its body is like smoked crystal, vanishing in the shadowy waters, letting sunlight pass straight through.

I hope to one day find the time and resources to track *segmenta* on the Congo River until I witness it meet another of its species—to study its behaviour and potential pair dynamics, perhaps even document the species mating. Yet while I am always particularly excited about interactions between mermaids, simply learning more about how exactly *segmenta* navigates the different ecosystems of the river and ocean landscapes will be rewarding beyond measure.

Sirenology has the capacity to teach our scientific community so much about how the earth functions if we only let ourselves be in awe of these creatures instead of rationalizing away their existence. We need to remain as adaptive in our thinking as *segmenta* is in its physique.

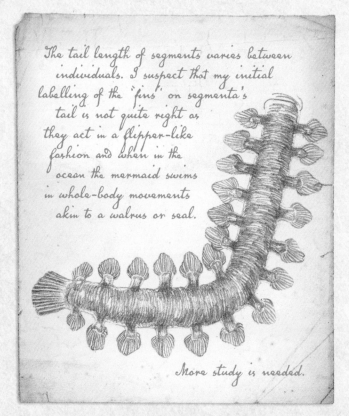

The tail length of segmenta varies between individuals. I suspect that my initial labelling of the 'fins' on segmenta's tail is not quite right as they act in a flipper-like fashion and when in the ocean the mermaid swims in whole-body movements akin to a walrus or seal.

More study is needed.

FURTHER READING

This is a list of works, some of them my own, foundational to the growing field of sirenology. This list is by no means a complete record of all the works and sources available on the subject; however, by including it I hope to impress upon you the importance of this realm of study and my work in particular.

Benzaquen, S. *Evidence of Vestige Gills in Coastal Simians*. New York: Pharynx Books, 1962.

LeBlanc, T. *Diving Bradycardia and the Mammalian Response to Aquatic Immersion*. BIOS University Press, 1972.

Lillefisk, Cecilia. *The curious case of the abandoned mermaid*. In Cobalt: Sea Witch or Mermaid, edited by Archibald Gilman, 61-72. Cleveland: Oceanographics Ltd., 1995.

———. *Plastic baggage: Ocean pollution and the sirens*. London: Waning Gibbous, 2000.

———. *Planets and sirens: Names and discoverers from the 15th century*. In Gazetteer of Marine Nomenclature, USGS Marine Biology. New York: Seafarers Press, 1998.

———. *Mastbound — Sirenological Lessons from Odysseus*. London: Waning Gibbous, 2002.

Lilly, John C, and David Chayefsky. *Exploration of ancestral memories triggered by prolonged sensory deprivation*. Brunswick, Maine: New English Journal of Psychology, 1978.

Morgan, Elaine. *The aquatic ape*. New York: Stein & Day Publishers, 1982.

Morgan, Francis. *Archaeological evidence of the existence of mer-simians on Easter Island and their unique adaptations*. Arkham, Essex County, Massachusetts: Miskatonic University Press, 1928.

Pimienta, E. *The Appearance of Subcutaneous Caudal Fin Forms in Extinct Primates of the Iberian Peninsula*. London: Morpho Press, 1974.

Straker, Trevor. *Seafarer's Accounts and Encounters with Marine Primates* 14, 2nd ed., 14:4–45. Bridgetown: Natural History Bulletin of the Caribbean, 1904.

ABOUT the AUTHOR

DR. CECILIA LILLEFISK is most definitely a real person. She simply values her privacy. She is also very busy travelling the world, researching mermaids, and writing her numerous bestselling books. In fact, they are so bestselling that copies are always out of stock. Some of her most popular titles include *The curious case of the abandoned mermaid*, *Plastic baggage: Ocean pollution and the sirens*, and *Mastbound — Sirenological Lessons from Odysseus*.

JANA HEIDERSDORF is a fantasy and horror illustrator with no life skills apart from drawing mermaids. Therefore it's a good thing Dr. Lillefisk discovered her during a research excursion to Berlin.

WOOL of BAT
a book from
EYE of NEWT
BOOKS